CLACKAMAS LITERARY REVIEW

2024
Volume XXVIII

Clackamas Community College
Oregon City, Oregon

CLR

CLACKAMAS LITERARY REVIEW

Managing Editor

Matthew Warren

Associate Editors

Jennifer Davis   Allison A. deFreese   Randy Murphy

Nicole Rosevear   Amy Warren

Assistant Editors & Designers

Allie Browning   Rosalyn Fullington   Josue Gutierrez

Tiyana Kohout   Zelda Merlin Stroup

Cover Art

Untitled by Melvin Louis Fessler

The Clackamas Literary Review is published annually at Clackamas Community College. Manuscripts are read from September 1st to December 31st. By submitting your work to *CLR*, you indicate your consent for us to publish accepted work in print and online. Issues I–XI are available through our website; issues XII–XXVII are available on our Submittable, and through your favorite online bookseller.

Clackamas Literary Review
19600 Molalla Avenue, Oregon City, Oregon 97045
ISBN: 978-1-7320333-6-8
Printed by Lightning Source
www.clackamasliteraryreview.org

CONTENTS

POSSIBILITY

PROSE

Editors' Note

Adaptation is the very center of survival, the power of all life. Like roots burrowing deeper into the ground and branches stretching towards the sky, life grows to survive in even the most hostile environments. The strongest trees may bend in the wind, but they are tough to break. When boulders block water's path, trickling rills swell until they cut through rock. Rather than resist change, we embrace it, gaining courage and resilience.

However, survival is not guaranteed; pain and loss are inescapable. When dense fog rolls in and swallows the sun, many of us will lose our way and become lost in the shadows. But our ability to adapt, to learn, can illuminate a new path forward. When we are able to follow it and emerge from the darkness, we do so stronger, wiser.

We at the *Clackamas Literary Review* invite you to explore these tales of adaptation and perseverance. Within these pages, we hope you find your reason to keep moving forward, through the dark and into light.

The Neanderthal in Me

Devon Balwit

My foremothers got up early to scrape and brew,
and I continue the tradition. My visiting children
know to expect the huff of yoga, pans
clattering, mere hours after they've gone to bed.
Sound travels unimpeded in a house with few
doors. A late start means hours wasted.

The poems that bubble up before dawn serve
as a reservoir into which I dip at work whenever
the class clock slows, tinkering with a verse,
adding or subtracting lines. Scientists suppose
a measurable advantage from this as our ancestors
journeyed north, learning to survive in snow.

What a long relay these genes have run to land
in me, protecting me from predators and pathogens.
Some as yet unborn grandchild will be given
the same baton, awakening long before
her siblings and using the quiet dark to tend
the strange fire she rekindles in her core.

Oakness

Derek R. Smith

The overground roots of the ancient oak
Reach upward toward the yearning moon
While subterranean branches
Collect their confidence
From a murky mineral earthen sky.
When strong winds prove insistent
The impossible weight and
Complex of this organism
Restates itself the oldest,
Most distinguished southern senator,
Made of phylum and bark.
Each season of the year floats along,
Mere window dressing seasonality
Though this Quercus alba,
Is an ancient ringed-column
Holding out for something sunnier.
Do we measure her by her excessive height
Or judge her by the comfort coolness
Her shadow provides in depth of summer sweating?
This grand oak only knows to grow
To continue standing in
The baby nursery where either

Her dedicated parent or some forgetful uncle squirrel
Deposited her.
Either way a seed dispersal agent left its mark back then
When growth was inches not decades.
She lays down miles of roots
Ensuring if she ever falls,
It's not for lack of hugging tight to earth.
She takes her space,
Reclaims her time,
And pushes forth, alive,
With no respect for bedrock.
This oak and to a lesser degree
Also elm and walnut,
They create a mezzo world
A third space
That collects what's good and admirable
From the sky and from the earth as well.

At the Mouth of Ross Island Lagoon

Eric le Fatte

If the fish at dusk
leapt out of the river
to swallow the moon,
she left a white crescent
and circles of ripples
that ran through the water.

I couldn't be sure
of her kind or her color,
but I'd choose enchanted
and scales of silver
if I had the choice.

The bridges and city
of lights in the distance
flashed in her eyes
like fragments of fables
as scarlets and golds of the sky
embellished her tail and fins.

If she jumped after insects
or merely for pleasure
I'd call that sufficient.
If she came to grant wishes
I'd say I've seen mine.

Hermana

(original poem from The Dickinson Archive,
Spanish language, Argentina)

María Negroni

Vinnie dice que le tengo fobia a la eternidad, que no hago más que llevarme la contingencia a la boca, y allí amarla con la arrogancia de la humildad. Dice que mi mente no vuelve al hogar jamás—ni siquiera refunfuñando—y que prefiero educar jilgueros desde la almohada, cuando mi pensamiento está incierto. Si digo que se equivoca, miento. Si digo que no, también.

Sister

(translated poem, English language)

Allison A. deFreese (translator)

Vinnie says I fear eternity, that I do nothing but lift possibility to my lips—and love it with an arrogant humility. She says my mind never comes home—not even with grumbling reluctance—that I prefer teaching goldfinches from my pillow when my thoughts are uncertain. If I say she's mistaken, I'd be lying. If I say she isn't—I would be, too.

Newborn

Pattabi Seshadri

I look at my newborn and think
of situations
that would test my devotion—
intruders, kidnappers, animal attacks.
I imagine that with each kiss
a malignant cell in my body splits
and measure my fear.

Sometimes I think about her
too much, look at her too long
and forget the simple things:
pulling the car seat straps
tight to her chest,
holding the back of her head,
washing my hands
before touching her.

I am in love with her
but I don't know her.
She smiles at me, but it's a reflex.

Still, I want her forever like this:
frog belly, bowlegs,
hairy back, jellyfish face,
black eyes staring at the space
behind my head.

That Kind of Love

Emma Snyder

The air was always stuffy and stale in Ma's house, even straight from the source. I spent my childhood summers holding my face above the window unit, trying to suck in the promise of cold it held. Ma would tell me I needed to suck in my stomach too, as I got older and age caught up to me. She said a flat stomach and a pretty face was the only way to catch a man who would pay my way, just as Pa did her. I practiced this philosophy for a short while, ages 10 to 14. I would catch my breath where my skin pulled taunt against each rib and hold it until a match struck fire in my lungs. It was all for nought in the end. Once Pa left and took his paychecks with him, the hunger sucked my stomach dry.

On more than one occasion in the years that followed, I asked Ma why Pa had left. Her answer was always the same; she'd tell me how she lost his love with time, that no man could love a woman who had traded beauty for age. When I looked at Ma, at the crow's feet around the corners of her eyes, the creases furrowed deep in her cheeks from every smile, and the silver hairs spun into her curls, I couldn't understand how she'd lost a thing.

My Ma held the two of us together after Pa left, sinned to keep meals on our table, and made me swear to stay beautiful, since she had never known another way to keep somebody's love. When I reached my twenties, I witnessed her unravelling. The arthritis ate away where each of her bones touched, and dementia curdled every coil in her brain until there was nothing left. In the same way she fought for us before, she clung to life until the end of it all, a shell of herself trapped in painful, confused consciousness.

On her very last day, I laid next to her on the hospital bed and ran my fingers through silver curls of hair long gone gray. She had been asleep for days by then, so I didn't know if she could still hear me. Either way, I told her I was grateful, that I finally understood what she had suffered through. I knew how fiercely she fought for my future, how many things she had dreamed for me to become, and I promised her that I would become them all.

In the years that followed her passing, I caught myself a man. He promised he would still love me when my beauty was gone, when my stomach was sagging and scarred from bringing life to our children. It took me a long while to learn that he meant it, that the soft parts of my belly didn't need to be sucked in, and the places on my body aged by time wouldn't scare him away.

Years more have passed, and now he's standing in front of our friends and family and a priest, swearing with the world as his witness that he will love me just the same as today when I am old and useless and ill, when I need someone to love me more than I ever have before, when I have nothing left to give. It makes me think of my Ma in that moment, of her never having that kind of love from somebody besides me.

When it's my turn, I promise it back to him, and I mean every word.

Sonnet for Post-divorce Photosynthesis

Riley Danvers

I look at my hands and
wonder if they were once saplings.
    A destiny of silk against the wind,
an anthem of furtive soil tended by silence.
Until these truths set me free,   I will
carry them between fingers and under
hair follicles, behind my eyes and in
my lungs.   There is
violence in the truth of un tend ed bro k en ness. The
caw and crone of crows in October drizzle
reminds me   I will always be the girl
with mycelium at my feet. Branch
is anthem; leaf is obituary, and   I
am a tower of budding declarations.

Self-portrait

Linda Drach

—for Traci Brimhall

In my next life, I'll skip work
when I'm sick. I'll skip through puddles
in silk pajamas, slip in and out
of midlife's boneyard lamplit
and amuleted. I'm happy now
just to be included. Next time,
I won't sprawl like a fat rhino
in the shade of ancient willow—waiting,
contented—a still, shallow hollow
where nothing much happens. I won't
swap stories of forever, as tiny horses
sniff the air and stamp their toes
in terror. I'll love like I know
it's the last days. I'll love with my talons
unmuffled by cottons. Unafraid
to be too sharp or too loud or too much
too often. I'll dangle tassels of starlight
over my scars. I'll live beehived
and velveteened. A burning cathedral.
A flowering spire feasting on ash.

Markings

Jeanine Stevens

The red fox on my January calendar
like a dream of winter—
cinnamon fur matching dried weeds,
snow reflecting the white ruff below his chin

In a haze, mountains pierce
a russet sky. Fuzzy clouds,
like empty squares hold promise,
no omens yet;
anything possible.

I pencil in two entries: a trip to the foothills
to deliver old photos to the Indian Rancheria,
and a writing session at Bread of Life.

Yesterday, walking my road in the fog,
I was startled by abrupt flight—
soaring like a shore bird,
pointed beak, long tail, curved neck, something
of cormorant, perhaps a stray
from the Pacific Flyway?

Am I ready for these brief distractions;
should I leave days open
    for the unexpected,
        even the glorious?

I wish all squares would hold good,
like last January, you completed chemo,
we enjoyed folk music at the Wild Eye Pub.

Somewhere in Quebec, the fox moves,
small steps marking his snow
filling his day with caution.

From the Notebooks of Myself, on the Occasion of Nothing, April, 2003

Craig Beaven

On a Tuesday in April in 2003
(my journal records)
I stopped writing a poem
mid-line
and the next line of the lined
notebook paper begins
(paragraph indent)
broke off for lunch
with Amy then
had the best sex
of my life,
and the next line
resumes the poem
I was working on.

The poem
was about
Emerson. Lunch
was probably Akida,
just two short blocks
away. I thought Emerson

had the answers. Every season
there was someone new,
an idea that would save me.

The only important details
about Emerson
are forgetfulness and fire:
all the words he wrote and lined up
in the notebooks—filling an entire
library of his home—
burned. And then he forgot
everything, including
the name of his wife.
It's the only part of his story
that matters, and I never learned it.

The impulse
to record
and remember.
There isn't an art
to it, unless cognition
is an art,
unless thinking
is a metaphor.
I'm 46 today.
46 winters.
It seems like more.
And I'll have to burn
all these journals

at the end. I measured
the stack last week—over
5 feet high.
Maybe when I'm dying,
if I have a year, the way
they sometimes give notice,
maybe I can reread
each one, can see
what happened
and how I felt. *The best*

sex of my life, Tuesday, April 8,
2003. One other thing
about Emerson: before
the two fires took every word—
the literal fire and the fire
of time—60 years before,
his first wife
died, and twice he went
to her tomb
and opened
the lid
to see.

What's with all the brutalist libraries?

Michael J. Galko

Sure, sure, libraries do not design themselves.
And there's nothing being sold within and only
so much money in the civic budget to foster
literacy (brutalism, after all, is easy on budgets).
So if you want to house a few million books
then get your concrete and glass and rebar out.
This past summer I was in Toronto, where the massive
Robarts Library takes up a whole city block
with the largest collection of books in North America.
And it reminded me of the LBJ Presidential Library
at UT Austin (my alma mater), which is a giant
stone slab with teeny black windows at the top.
My daughter and I took a jaunt to Mexico City
in the fall and, by accident, stumbled across
the Vasconcelos Library which from the front looks like
a baleen whale scooping up the krill of all published books,
and from the inside looks like a place where Job
could have roamed the suspended glass-floor stacks
for as long as God would imprison him (in a strange
inversion there is even a whale skeleton hanging inside).
And then I remembered the Geisel Library
(yes that Geisel—Dr. Seuss) on the UCSD campus

with its cantilevered platforms of glass and gray.
There are more: Rensselaer, University of Chicago,
Northwestern, Oberlin's Mudd Library (where my
older daughter studies), University College Dublin.
It is strange to me that this architectural movement
originally spawned by Mussolini's desire for permanent
monumental structures, structures that impose
and dominate, structures that shake a fist at transience
(hence the brutal name), would be adopted by later
architects to enshrine the books the fascists would burn.
Maybe that is the point. To make it seem like these vast citadels
of accumulated knowledge are indeed impregnable—
can withstand the idea, or even the fact,
of our ongoing barbarian backslide.

Role Reversal

Devon Balwit

—for Maeve

If I were Picasso, and this graphite-scratched face
intentional, I'd be a genius. Instead, I wince
as the teacher leans in to look. I wait for her
to alight on the root of the problem. When I offer
my pencil, a few strokes are all it takes
to make my work less orthognathic.
Now, I am out of the woods, and can add shade,
the dark terminator line, shadows that fade
into white. Class ends, and I wash my hands
of the muddle they've made. With one last look
at the bust on its ramshackle plinth, I pack up.
The teacher praises my effort, and I understand
how my own students feel as they close their books
on a language that slyly evades their grasp.

Notes from a Minor Poet

—A review of William Jolliff's collection *At Rest in My Father's House* (Aubade Publishing, 2022).

Jake Bienvenue

When these poems were first given to me in the fall of 2018, I think the poet, William Jolliff, had little hope they would ever become a book. I could not understand why. I announced my plan to review his unpublished masterpiece—just something, I said humbly, to get him over the edge, provoke some groundswell, attract some publishers. Then I went home and wrote an extremely bland close reading of the book which was both totally shapeless as well as more-or-less critically inept. I was 21, his student.

Four years later, when I heard it was to be released by Aubade Publishing—a publishing house in the most literal sense, consisting of a husband, a wife, their two daughters—I pre-ordered the book and considered the intervening time. Four years ago, I'd been an idiot. Now, I was a man. I would fulfill my obligation to the book. Wasn't I now more capable? But when my copy arrived, I found myself jotting down the very things I'd written the first time—banal observations on the book's structure, overzealous estimations of its technical prowess, perhaps more enlightened comments on cadence and meter, but overall an underwhelming analysis which fell very short of how I felt about it. My analysis was unconvincing even to me. I wondered whether there was anything special about it at all.

For reassurance, I opened Goodreads—a terrible idea. At the time of writing, there are 16 reviews of *At Rest in My Father's House.* Most were written by people who received galley copies. One wonders how many copies there are in the world, in the hands of readers. 100? 200? How do you discuss a work that is more important to you than it is to the world? It's like talking to yourself: you worry if you do it too much it'll become a habit. A review presumes its own importance, as well as that of its subject. But what does it matter to review a book practically no one will read in a literary magazine no one will read? Some honesty, it seems, is necessary. We're chatting amongst ourselves, at best. And yet it was this irrelevance, this paradigm of meaninglessness, which provided the entry point for the only reading of *At Rest in My Father's House* that does the poems any justice.

Part one begins, "Long before I was born, / the glory left the barns," (6). We begin with vacancy. In the poet's Ohio, corn prices are down, Vietnam is underway, the land is soaked with chemicals, God and the father are distant, and the chosen are in exile. The setup is ripe for an Old Testament prophet. Yet rather than condemnation or warning, Jolliff offers a beatific vision of this hinterland and its people. Central to this vision is the paradox of irrelevance. This appears throughout the collection in the form of the meaningless gesture. Routinely and obsessively, these men and women perform actions which accomplish nothing. In "Cards on the Farm," the poet details the importance a game of cards can assume to those whose lives are dictated by things outside their control. He asks, "Why not / smoke another Lucky, eat another piece of pie, / deal another hand? Why not enjoy a raucous / chance on something that doesn't really matter?" (25). The anxiety of agricultural life is displaced into the game. This displacement recurs throughout the collection: here in a man who shoots stop signs, there in a man who reloads countless 12-gauge shells before he dies and leaves his sons thousands of rounds stacked in crates. The most obvious example is farming itself. Why continue a way of life industrial-scale agriculture has rendered unprofitable and thus, at least economically, meaningless? These poems vibrate with the tension of their own irrelevance. The question Jolliff asks of us, of his characters, is summed up in a poem which invokes the poet Wendell Berry. In "The Way My Father Farmed," Jolliff acknowledges that "[t]he way my father farmed / was hell on women and good horses, and one / of the women was the earth herself" (18). Yet he asks, "But was there some blessedness, / too, in all that persistent attention," (18)?

This serves as the book's operant question, and its poems constitute attempts at an answer. In its tight, old-school metric, in its repeated formal decisions, and in its overall structure, *At Rest in My Father's House* is, if nothing else, persistently attentive. Nearly every poem is at least roughly iambic, such that it seems as if the poet composed in iambic pentameter, then jumbled and broke the lines to conceal it. The stanza formation, too, is highly regular—mostly couplets, tercets, or quatrains in repeating combinations. Flip rapidly through the book and you'll see lines and stanzas of such regularity they resemble rows of corn seen from the air. Likewise, the book's structure is tightly organized. The collection progresses through four parts. Part one details childhood, innocence, then departure. Parts two and three explore the mundanity and struggle of the men and women of rural Ohio. Part four follows the poet from farming to professorship in Oregon, then finally tracks his return, through the mnemonic of poetry, to childhood. What blessedness the characters, as well as the poet, do not find in circumstance, in change in fortune, they find in repetition, in structure.

While some of these poems never cross into revelation ("First Snow" and "A Boy and His Dog" come to mind), many culminate in small but profound moments of illumination, if not outright beauty. This illumination is built into the prosody itself. Jolliff repeatedly employs a particular formal strategy to transport the reader into these small blessings. Because the stanza is rarely varied, any departure from the structure of the poem becomes laden with meaning. Often, these departures are epiphanic in nature. For example, "John Deere Green" consists of 10 roughly pentametric couplets followed by a one-line stanza, the zinger: "cleaning brushes in the emerald stones of the yard" (14). The final image is separated from the formal architecture of the poem; the ending comes as a surprise, a revelation; the stones are alight in the color of another world. If that line were tacked onto the end of a couplet, the effect would be lost, the image would lose some portion of its glow. Same thing a few poems later, in "The Grip:" six quatrains before the ghostly final line. "The Old Ways" and "Brother Everest Cleans His .22s" follow more-or-less the same pattern, and a number of others follow a similar principle, ending either with a floating couplet or a related formal break. It is the regularity of the form which allows for these sudden shifts into revelation. In other words, the regularity, banality, even, becomes a necessary precondition for the poetic departure. While this may constitute a somewhat puritanical aesthetic, these poems find and evoke a sense of rest in their own regularity, as well as in the surprising breaks from it.

What I find not only moving but convincing about this collection is its persistence, not only within its own technique, but in regards to the collective ennui which seems to dwarf the discipline of poetry as a whole. What the poet has drawn from farming he applies later to poetry. This is the book's gift, its vision, its rest. These poems teach us to treasure those things no one treasures, to privilege the apparently meaningless. In this way the poet speaks to the broader condition in which we in the literary community find ourselves. From these poems, from these lives, a few iambs of blessing.

We Live in Four Rooms

Chuck Carlise

We live in four rooms,
the two of us, the tumble
of us, paint splatter & high
ceilings, we pull & dissolve,
become one another, in tiny
flashes of light, endearments
quiet, bite marks on hips, oil
& sweat-fingers pressed
to every mirror, the fear & night-
haze of four rooms & all this
heart-pound fever of closeness,
midnight laughter, sleep-breathing
laced with nightmare, all
this danger, shared frustration—
shouting at each other at
three in the morning,
desperate to be heard,
hanging frantic to the last
shreds of self in the great
fade and scatter of these
rooms, of this night, of our
one flailing life we live

in this cell, you & I, drowning
as though we never had
a choice, as though there had never
been anything more important
in both of our pitiful lives than this,
these rooms, these words,
this whiplash of fury & dread,
blind exasperation—*Love*
reach for me, for god's sake, please—
& the house breathes,
contracts, it closes in but
pulls us apart—I want
to lay my head in your lap,
to laugh at our frayed
edges, to sing to you from
a doorway across these four
rooms, these chambers that keep
us warm & soft, it's not
a weakness to wait, to sit,
to let these walls hold us,
these skylights, dark floorboards,
the pedestal sink, these four
rooms are all we are,
& all we've been—shredded
paper scraps, bobby pins,
longing & resentment we'll
never confront, just carry & chafe—
it surrounds us every day
here in these four rooms where

we live, where we sleep, where
we hate & hold each other; these
four rooms we'll burn to the
ground one day when it hurts
too much to hang on;
the four rooms we'll lose
& never get back & regret
letting go for
the rest of our lives.

The Roses

Kelleen Zubick

June in a car with you, without air
conditioning, in something cheap
like an Opal, low to the ground
with black vinyl seats. Fast
enough to make wind roar
and my hair fan about
the passenger side, the open
beer between my thighs
sweating and darkening my jeans
as if something more serious
were happening and not just us,
barely friends, being not quite lost,
exchanging overpass with bridge
back and forth on Storrow Drive
between Cambridge and the
Prudential Center, lamenting
plans to put out the Citgo sign.
What we did and did not know—
your studies at Sanskrit, my poetics,
our sandwich shop jobs after
graduation and after other friends
flew to their real homes and we

discovered we didn't have much
to get back to, driving interchanges
like a track car until I stopped
laughing and your talk ran out
and I sat too close, my damp singlet,
and you pulled over just streets off
Plow and Stars, and we had to walk
or else sink in rising desire,
the way the scent of those roses
along the chain link in the dark
was fixating, was splintering
to the opacity of night. Then
your hands in my hair, wrapping
in its length, so close I can see
you mouthing, *roses roses*
roses, like a canticle, before
I tore the air to reach you.

Snack Cakes

Ace Boggess

Why does midnight sink its spear in my side,
say *Sweets*, say *Now*
you must fill me with emptiness?

I go to the cabinet without
thinking, grab the white-iced white,
zebra-striped, birthday-sprinkled.

Hunger is a word with many meanings.
Midnight calls to all of them:
peanut-butter bar for substance,

the occasional orange for lust.
I want what I want, &
maybe what I want is my destruction,

the lover for an hour
with no exchange of names.
It's that, hearing the package tear,

hands doing what they do,
not caring what
they put in my mouth in the dark.

The Red Hat

Lee Varon

Fortunately, I suppose, I was able to recuperate at my brother's house on the Cape. He has a place on the lower Cape where all the hoity-toity bastards flocked after Covid hit the cities.

After my fever broke, I began to go for walks along the shore. It was nearly autumn, and the sky was utterly clear most days. The air crisp. Only a touch of chill. Most days though, I just sat on his wide deck. I found his binoculars hanging on a coatrack and, often, I'd take them and gaze out at the sea, the dilapidated jetty jutting out from the beach, or sometimes at the neighboring houses. Nobody could see me—I learned long ago how to become invisible. I huddled down in an Adirondack chair in my gray windbreaker and was at least two hundred fifty yards from any other house. I spent my days like that, and reading the books my brother had scattered around. *The Time Machine. The Adventures of Robinson Crusoe. Frankenstein.* Mostly classics. Randolph always fancied himself an intellectual. Actually, the books were all in a fake leather-bound series and I could tell, by the crack of the spine as I opened each, he'd never read any of them.

Like I said, it's pretty deserted out here. Especially now that summer's coming to an end. It's still hot according to the thermometer but, after Covid, I seem to feel cold all the time. Supposedly, I'm not contagious or anything but I still wear a mask when I go into town to buy supplies. I wasn't sorry when people started wearing masks—no one would recognize me. Town is about twenty minutes down a wind-ing sandy road. There's a small grocery store, a bookstore, a trinkets shop, the usual real estate office, and a single café. I like this part of the Cape. Fewer tourists milling around. Randolph hardly ever comes down. I'm not even sure why he bought the place except to add another feather to his cap. The man with everything, golden boy Randolph. No doubt, Father, if he were still alive, would be proud of his younger son. That's right. Randolph is younger than me by 18 months. People always mistook him for my older brother because of his larger size.

Most of the people that came down from Boston and New York have left by now. The old retirees remain. Like the people next door. The old couple is still here and all week their two grandkids have also been here. I assume they are their grandkids. Two girls. The older maybe about ten and the younger eight or so. I try not to look at them, to continue reading this chapter of *Robinson Crusoe*. But they keep dis-tracting me as they play out on the dilapidated jetty or walk up and down the beach collecting shells. It's clear they don't get along. More about that later.

Today, the wind is bringing the familiar unwelcome hint of fall. Yet the sun warms me when it pierces the clouds and I bask in its warmth, wishing I never had to return to the city, those staring neighbors who've seen me on the registry. I adjust the binoculars. An expensive pair of Vipers 10x42. The beach is deserted except for the girls. I'm sure they can't see me, yet it's remarkable how clearly I can see their expressions from where I sit undetected. Apparently, they're alone although the waves are rougher today and an east wind is blow-ing darker clouds ashore. The taller, stockier girl wears a black dress and holds a cranberry red crocheted hat. The smaller girl wears a red dress that hangs loosely on her thin frame. I don't often see little girls in dresses. Both have dark hair and I assume they're sisters. Maybe something terrible happened to their parents and they suddenly had to be sent to stay with their grandparents. The bigger girl has a habit of taking the red hat and twirling it around her fingers in a kind of teasing gesture. Sometimes, she throws it in the air and the smaller girl tries, and repeatedly fails, to catch it. It makes me wonder if the hat belongs to the smaller girl, and her sister has stolen it from her and is taunting her. The girl in black also has a habit of leaning over the rusted railings along the jetty and beckoning the smaller girl to follow. But as soon as the smaller girl does, her sister runs to the opposite side of the rocks. As she does this, she tosses her head from side to side, and red highlights in her hair reflect the sun like metal blades.

I enjoy watching them, knowing they're unaware of my presence. In fact, I've always enjoyed watching children from afar when they don't know I'm watching. Eventually, I see that the smaller girl is growing more and more tired and frustrated; I can tell by her heaving shoulders that she's crying. I can tell by her mouth, open wide, that she's screaming something at her tormentor. Words that are lost in gusts of sea breeze, the screech of gulls overhead. Finally, she sinks down into a disheveled lump, hands covering her eyes. Above her, as though egged on by this collapse, the taller girl starts skipping in circles, her sun-tanned legs kicking blithely in the air; and she seems to be singing—perhaps some nursery rhyme. Yes, I remember... "Jack be nimble, Jack be quick." Randolph often sang that song. "Be quick be quick, be quick." I was not an athlete like Randolph. I was never quick. At an early age, Father stopped expecting much from me. Randolph went on to win ribbons and trophies that Father displayed in a glass case.

I wondered, at this point, if I should intervene, yet I hesitated. After all, where were the grandparents? I felt a sudden fury that they'd put me, of all people, in this predicament. If I did intervene, wouldn't they wonder why I'd noticed their grandchildren playing? They might even ask: Why was I watching? How long had I been watching and so on. I knew where questions like that could lead. And somehow, things might get back to Randolph. He might forbid me from ever coming down here again.

I thought the girls would stop playing, but they didn't. At the continued taunts of her persecutor, the small girl in red, wiping her tears away with her forearm, rose and ran to the other side of the jetty like a streak of lightning as the red hat on the bigger girl bobbed back and forth like an apple. She took the hat off, twirled it around on her fingers, and once again they began their capers, yet now I was sure that the small girl was forcing this sudden display of gaiety. It was too enthusiastic to be genuine.

The sun was beginning to set and, between dark clouds, streaks the color of pomegranate filled the sky; yet the children continued their play with the same energy as before—the smaller desperately attempting to follow the larger. How innocent this scene would look to a stranger coming upon it. I wondered how many times such painful scenes had occurred in the past. I winced recalling the many evenings our parents had left my brother and me alone. "Here's a phone number if you need us," my mother would say, plunking the number beneath the fire engine magnet on the refrigerator. Of course, we knew better than to call. Our parents were playing cards, or shopping, or who knows where. They weren't at a place where they expected to be disturbed. Once, I'd called in tears pleading with them to return home because Randolph had hung me upside down off our balcony; my father simply laughed and hung up the phone.

Over by the jetty where the railing was beginning to crumble, I noticed a sudden disturbance. My hands began to shake uncontrollably. It was as if I sensed what was about to happen as the larger girl leaned dangerously over the railing waving the red hat, and the little girl lunged, finally grabbing the hat. Did her sister lurch away from her and fall? There was a splash like a tarpon arching away from a hook. Or did I imagine a splash? Below the jetty, the girl in black bobbed up, was felled by a swelling wave, and disappeared. I stared as the little girl crumpled the hat to her small chest, looking down into the waves as her sister desperately flailed at the frothy waves, trying to stay afloat. Standing there in the twilight, the smaller girl made no motion to run to the house, her red dress barely visible in the coming night.

I, also, was unable to move. For a long time, I sat deeply in the low chair clutching the binoculars. The gulls screeched overhead; I shut my eyes against a sudden gust of salty air. When I opened them, the girl's form stood motionless until night ate her in layers and she was gone.

I blinked into the growing darkness—few houses, no stores. No playground. No daycare center. No park. No school. It was meant to be a *safe* place. A place I could recuperate away from the crowded group home with the snoring of other desperate men who had given up on tomorrows.

My hands shook as I pushed myself up from the Adirondack chair. I was afraid I would faint. I felt weak, but suddenly, also, energized. I knew I needed to leave immediately. I grabbed some cheese and bread and a little yogurt for the ride. I returned *Robinson Crusoe* to its shelf. As I drove down the winding road, terrified my tires would begin to spin in the sand, I noticed the lights had come on in the grand-parent's house and their figures could be seen frantically rushing from room to room. No doubt, the police had been called. As I drove past the house, I saw the girl in red at the end of their driveway, still clutching the hat. I had to pass very close to her and as I did, I caught her eyes. She stared as if she had seen me before. As if she recognized me. I tried to look away, at the side or rearview mirror, but I felt trapped by her gaze.

By the time the police come, I'll be on Route 6 headed back into town.

Unfortunately, I wouldn't get to see the movie I'd chosen from my brother's vast collection—one of those film noirs where something in you, in spite of everything, always ends up rooting for the bad guys.

Going to America

Git Lanza

Monday night.
Rain.
A teenage girl—
face brown,
hair matted, wet,
a baby in her arms—
limped up to my gate.
Are you from America?
Are streets there of gold?
she asked and begged for coins.
I gave her some
told her yes
the streets are made
of gold

then went inside

but suddenly heard
a scream
and rushed out
to investigate.

Two cops were standing
over her
threatening her with clubs
demanding her
identity card
which she didn't have.
They tore the baby
from her arms
tossed her in
the back of a van
and sped away.

Friday night.
Rain.
The same girl with crutch
standing at my gate.
She begged for coins and said
I'm going to America
where everyone is rich.

Class

Dion Farquhar

You'll always be a Marxist at heart
wielding the kerosene
because you've been *poor*
(not the middle-class *broke* you are now)
lived the prison of 9-to-5
making barely enough
to pay the rent, Con Ed, Bell
little left over to buy
      a treat from the bakery
      for your dying mother
      on her birthday
      in the hospital
      or a burger at night
      with friends after class
stuck, reduced, ground down

the mystery is that
there's no *one* to blame
it's nothing personal
just systems and relations
dominating most of us

which you learn
the gory details about in grad school

you know it's no use
trying to smash something
or putting a bullet in a boss
or setting something on fire
but at least you've got this poem

Prophecy Poem

Scott T. Starbuck

At some point even banks
and cell towers died.
Grocery shelves
and gas pumps emptied.

We were hungry,
tired, and worried.
We met in makeshift
churches with candles.

Without street lights
constellations appeared,
starting conversations
and bringing joy.

Some talked about
Legend of Unmarked Snow
far up north
while bravest left to find it.

we're a car(t)nation

Abbie Doll

no winter landscape I that's even I a smidge suburban I is complete
without I a shopping cart I alone -&- forsaken I yes I **but!** I in better
condition I than most I abandoned folk I -&- by that i mean I still
upright I still atop wheels I that function still I despite being nowhere
near I a store I as if this I boxy pack mule I waltzed out I did a jail-
break sprint I for the american (day)dream

the cart's a staple I commodity I in these rural I communities I —a re-
gional specialty! I here I try our fried bologna I two I inch-thick slabs I
slapped atop bleached buns that I disintegrate in a glance I just come
to our hidden gem I train-car diner I IcIoIrInIfIiIeIlIdI adjacent I middle-
of-n o w h e r e complacent

we owe these unmanned carts I a great deal I (-&- no, i'm not talkin'
no costco *bogo*)

perhaps I a seussian series I devoted to this exploratory spirit I -&-
icy-trail spit I their lofty aspirations I translated to I whimsical illus-
trations I that capture their quirks: I their squeaky wheels - flyswatter
frames -&- capitalist subserviency

the cart is | *the* poster child | for the forlorn— | she's a ditched pup | bereft of cardboard | no box to contain | the whine | the wait | no bluster shield

she waits -&- waits -&- w(eigh)ts | on that next shopper | that next passerby | that next fido chance | to prove herself | lovable (-&-) home-worthy

or *maybe,*

we've got a hapless addict | cocked -&- loaded | ready to kill | for one last hit | of warmth | from gloved fingertips | grip-wrapped 'round | her stone-cold handlebar

she's out there | after all | in the o p e n | elements-exposed | a concrete fixture | here in our midwest horizon | where we'd take sepia-toned days | any day | over the bleak | barren | lifeless | flatness | of it all | the gray on gray on gray on gray

no one installed a break | so, | there's no stopping | her ambition | no halting | her delusions | no stopping | her [period] | she might just | roll right off | the lot | right into | that cloud-bath sunset | —that one | right there | below that concrete eyesore elephant-skin overpass

-&-

besides | who's to say | she won't win | won't conquer | all this muted grayscale | this depression-inducing apocalyptic terrain | with her ugly durability | ? |

she's a cockroach vehicle | bound to survive | waiting | plotting | bid-
ing her time | assessing -&- appraising | this— | her future domain |
everything the light touches | (as mufasa once enlightened) | except
our girl | would *survive* | that fall | survive that subsequent wildebeest
trample | hell she'd even join the stampede | -&- roll | right through
the ravine

~ happy as hell | just to be | along | for the ride ~

because carts | are pack animals | (too) | -&- lord do they get | that
empty pit— | those swiss-cheese gaps | that grief deposits | as it loots |
our fragile fleshy grids

World War One Mask

—from the 1918 photograph, *American Red Cross Studio of Portrait Masks in Paris*

E. Laura Golberg

An O, an outline of the earth where the mouth should be;
teeth, upper jaw, destroyed by a hand grenade.
 "Hideous is the only word for these smashed faces."
One man wouldn't let his mother see him.
Anna Coleman Ladd, sculptor, founded the studio,
adorned it with flags and flowers, drank tea
with her "faceless ones."
     She pushed back the hands of time
using photographs, or guesswork, to restore
what was crushed. She cut copper, hammered
it to cover the ruined face, now restored,
then colored the mask to match the skin.
The man wrote, "Thanks to you I can live again."
We all find ways.

It Still Comes to Mind

J Kramer Hare

Dad had cried at the makeshift Holocaust
    museum that our eighth-grade class had made.

It was comprised, mostly, of diaries:
    imagined artifacts, once held by hands

whose youth, whose hopes, whose warmth had been too brief.

    I will not tell you Dad conforms
        to that old trope, as well worn-out
    as a frontiersman's leather belt
        of bullets, or his Stetson hat:

the strong, stoic, silent male which movies
    have poised to win the plaudits of the crowd—

I will not say, *never had I witnessed*
    such wetness in his eyes; although he fronts

as a witty, risible, part-time prick—

who you'd hate to face off against
in a cross-examination,
who stands aloof when beggars voice
their joyless small demands—he is

at heart a sentimentalist. He'd scanned,
one by one, the books we'd crafted (in Art)

and filled in with our own versions (informed
by Social Studies) of what the victims

were made to suffer not so long ago—

I can't recall the personage
I'd chosen for my own account;
It was a girl, I know, and how
I'd cut the narrative upon

the boarding of the trains—feeling no right
to imagine what happened after that,

feeling that the best I could do was to
log the indignities of the ghetto—

these few points can I still remember well.

He'd scanned the books and shed his tears
      and told me what tremendous jobs
we all had done. And as I've said,
      it's no great shock to see him cry,

but those particular tears have lingered,
      refused to go dry in my memory—

much more so than any shed since—and when
      I picture him crying in the abstract

this is the image which still comes to mind.

      And when I feel like shedding tears
          for those whose sufferings I have
no right, even, to imagine,
          this image will still come to mind.

Before

Matthew Kohut

Near the end my father told me
about an evening long ago
as summer began to fade,

the last wisps of smoke rising from the grill,
my sister and I playing with him in the yard
until the final rays of sun disappeared,

a day that vanished when we fell asleep,
a snapshot he carried for forty years
of the moment before the fall.

Acorn

Travis Stephens

He gave me a wooden acorn
life-like, life sized
of a pale hard, wood
sanded, capped,
real in every way save
it was not oak,
once
or ever could be.
Why he gave me the acorn
I am not certain &
never asked
glad for any gift
from one I was so enamored of.
He is likely a father,
partner, happily distant
from past loves
one time lovers &
tiny, careless gifts.

The acorn lives in a tin box
a collection
of recollection.

With it a pin from a 5K
in Minnesota, garnet, agate,
a shell from Florida.
Ticket stubs.
Library card from Seattle,
a pot metal piece from an
ancient pickup that states
APACHE.
Why not Chippewa
why not Tlingit or Miwok?
Ask Ford, ask Chevy.
Or ask me, why keep any
of this stuff, casually known
as junk?
My stuff, not very important
& easily
misplaced, easily forgotten.

I found the box only
because we moved
from apartment to house.
My first, your latest.
Late nesters.
Gopher lawn, maybe garden,
extra bedrooms to fill.
Why not plant them all—
shell, stone, pickup seeds
& false acorn—

in the dirt,
to see which emerges
what fearful bit of symmetry?

Epistolary for the First Six Months after Her Death

Rosemarie Dombrowski

Dear cracks in the lamp, dear cracks in the veneer of everything, I'm not angry with the cats, but I need more quiet, a mass deletion of the inbox of lucid dreams and the race to rescue her, the regrets I can't let go of.

Dear menopause-induced sleep disturbances, dear depression and grief, I still can't accept that all life is suffering, or how our minds grow foggy and depraved, always wrestling with the next trauma— the liver resections and double mastectomies, the chemo pumps and schizophrenic episodes, all the things there may not be cures for, this parallel chart of pain.

Dear exsanguinated heart, I guess this is what it feels like to die and go on living, all the muted voices in the darkness, all the mutes living under one roof, all of us trapped on this side of the light.

Dear catechism, dear St. Francis Xavier and Cathedral schools, I hate you more than ever—your diminishments, your deficiencies in STEM, your rules about earrings and eyeliner. You've blackened my heart in the most radical ways, and for that I'm grateful. Still, you were mostly bullshit, and I've come back to tell you that there's nothing on the other side.

Smoke, Fire, Ashes

Ross West

Lucy Ann

The Lake Wontaka Lounge isn't as special as Dad said it would be, just a noisy bar and a bunch of tables and up at the front a little platform for the band. A little darker than I imagined. Mom says they play rockabilly music. I don't even know what that is. Why did we even come here? They told me like twenty-seven times how much fun we'd have, a family vacation up at the lake, how much I would just luuuuuuuv it. Right.

It takes the waitress like nineteen centuries to find us then she asks what I want and I say fruit juice and I'm thinking about the vitamins and antioxidants and she looks like a cow and Mom looks at me even cowier and I can tell she wants to lecture me about the calories. I know, Mom, I know you think I'm fat, but I don't care what you think. I'm going to drink what I want, okay? The waitress tells me what kind of fruit juice they have and it looks like I'm going to end up with cranberry. Not my favorite. I ask if it comes in a recyclable container and she says she doesn't know for sure but thinks maybe it comes in a plastic bottle. Oh yeah, real great, like I really want to kill the oceans for a sip of juice. Never mind. I have plain old water and Mom and Dad have their beer. Then Mom grabs Dad's hand and says, c'mon, let's dance, and he's like nah, nah, nah, can't we just listen? She gives him The Look and drags him out right in front of the band where everybody in the whole place can see. And they're dancing out there all by themselves. Oh god.

It's just too hideous to watch so I open my book. To read it, I have to hold it right next to the tiny little candle on our table. This chapter's horrifying, someplace up in Alaska all the ice is melting and there's this polar bear family starving to death.

I sniff Mom's beer and it smells like aquarium water. The singer up on the stage has a fancy jacket with sequins and embroidered roses and his guitar is yellow with gold sparkles. Dad lifts Mom's hand up and they make a little arch and she spins around under it. More couples are out there now—much better dancers. But look at them, all of them, dancing away la la la like the world isn't on fire. Wake up, dummies, there's no more time.

The singer kicks a bright red cowboy boot way up into the air and the drummer bashes the cymbals to finish the song. Dad comes back over to the table and Mom just stands out there, giving him the stink eye. He asks if I've had enough and I'm like, duh, yeah. Mom finally slinks over and they snap at each other and he tells her he's going to take me back up to the room.

Terry

I don't want to make a scene, spoil everything, so sure, okay Krys, we'll dance. Whatever Krys wants, Krys gets. The band's good and all—very good, in fact—but dancing swing, with Krys, at this particular time— it's just a little too much to fake. And look at Lucy, she's getting antsy. One song is plenty. One and done.

Lucy says she wants to go back to the room, and I ask Krys if she's ready to go. The music's so loud she can't hear, so I yell, *YOU WANNA GO?* She takes a good-sized hit off her beer and says she wants to stay and listen some more. Okay, sure, I'll take Lucy and probably come back in a little while. She's still mad about the dancing and makes a face like *Whatever*. I look around and Lucy's already halfway to the exit.

I catch her at the door and, outside where it's quieter, ask if she liked the music. She's her usual self, not saying much but obviously not impressed. At least she's not being openly hostile.

We walk down the hallway to the lobby—where that perky red-headed kid checked us into the resort this morning. He lit right up when I told him we had the Outdoor Fun Package, gave me a big toothy grin—felt like a good omen.

Did you like the kayaking, I ask. She shrugs. Did you get a little scared when the wind came up? Shrug. We made it all the way around the lake, didn't we? No response. She beelines to the elevator and pushes the button. We wait, my mind wanders...

Oh Daddy, I'm totally loving this vacation. You drove us over to this fancy resort, carried all our stuff up to the room, got us all geared up for the half-day, lunch-included kayak adventure. The windstorm, yeah, that was a little scary, but you led us to safety—an experience I will never forget. And you took us out for a wonderful Thai dinner where Mom even laughed at one of your jokes. And then we—

Ding, the elevator bell chimes. Lucy zooms inside and parks herself against the back wall, looks straight ahead clutching her book to her chest like a life preserver. When the doors open on our floor, she trots off, getting smaller and smaller as she moves down the long corridor of doors and more doors.

Krys saying, "I'm going over to my sister's—she's got a bad cold or the flu or something."

I feel around in different pockets for the room key.

And the next day Krys, like a goddam Mother Teresa, "Poor Patty"—so innocent, shaking her blonde head. "Whatever she's got, it's really holding on. Don't wait up, I might stay over."

I insert the key card into the little slot—*click*—and push the door open. The room is pitch black.

And me taking Patty get-well flowers, a surprise. Mr. Nice Guy. She opens her front door—healthy as a horse. Is Krys here? She has no idea what I'm talking about. Everything stops. Everything crumbles. And I'm standing there holding the bouquet, the world's biggest chump.

I flick on the light. Lucy wiggles past me, jumps onto her bed and bounces a couple of times. She says she's going to shower, gets her stuff.

I bunch the pillows against the headboard and check my phone. A message from Amanda. Ooh, now *that's* a selfie. Skimpy black bra, one hand cupping the back of her head, elbow high, bedroom eyes, puckered lips.

That first night, Amanda in her kittycat whisper, "I'm here to pamper you...anything you want." Her voice breathy and hot, right at my ear, in slips her tongue.

Lucy says something in the bathroom. I turn to listen, about to ask her *What?* Then I hear a few more chirpy sounds and figure she's just sort of singing or something.

Krys swears it was only once. *Oh, only once. Well, that's super great news. I guess everything's just a-okay then, huh?* No Krys, everything is not fucking okay.

She's begging—*Look, I understand, if you need to get back at me, even things up. Go ahead, find somebody. Do what you want.*

I stare at Amanda's picture, spread my finger and thumb on the phone's glass surface, zoom in, remember.

We have a couple of drinks on her sofa and Amanda stands up and unzips the tight little skirt and lets it drop around her bare feet. Looking at me over her shoulder, she thrusts out her hip, rests her hand on the curving haunch—the red thong's thin strap disappears into the crack of her ass.

I get home, Krys looks at me all mad and hurt and she starts right in with how she isn't as cool with the arrangement as she thought she was going to be. She wants to go to counseling.

Typical Krys. First I catch her red handed and she's bawling her eyes out—*anything, anything, just don't throw me out*—but when I have a little fun she sings a very different tune. Okay fine, we'll go to counseling. But you said that if I wanted to find somebody you'd understand, did you not? Okay. Don't forget that.

I told Krys I'd come back down to the lounge…but I don't know, it's been a long day. Tomorrow we're hiking up a mountain. I kick off my shoes and pull the comforter over my legs.

Lucy comes out of the bathroom and crawls into her bed, a small bump under the covers of the queen-size. She asks what I'm doing, and I say, oh, just catching up on my email. She says she's going to sleep, and I ask if she isn't going to read. No, the kayaking tired her out. Did you like being on the lake? She says it was cool then turns off the lamp by her bed. I switch off my lamp too and am lying there in the dark feeling pretty great about the kayaking when she says good night and I say good night Lucy Goosey and then she laughs her funny chipmunk laugh and says good night again and now we're playing the good-night game like we used to when she was little, repeating and repeating good night back and forth until she finally drifts off.

The couples' counselor says he believes we can make things work—but only if we want to. He looks a little less certain when Krys tells him about the blank check she wrote me as far as other relationships and how she wants to take it back. Then she tries to make me the bad guy for not dropping my extracurricular the second she felt a hundredth as bad as I felt when I found out about hers. The counselor doesn't buy her bait-and-switch bullshit, says he can't exactly bless my affair, but we should look at it as an intermediate hurdle on the way to better days.

At the second session the counselor suggests we reboot the relationship, take a test run as a happy family, go on a vacation. *And don't just gut it out, make a good-faith effort to have fun. If you're not having fun, together, as a family, what's the point?* He reminds us of the alternative, a divorce and shared custody of Lucy.

I look back at my phone and think maybe I'll just write Amanda a quick message to keep things bubbling along—maybe we could get together after work on Thursday. I see her picture with those luscious lips and I hear the counselor say *good-faith effort*. I look over where Lucy is sleeping and can just hear her soft little breaths. I scan around in the darkness, and I guess there must be a mirror on the opposite wall because there's my own face, illuminated in the bluish light of my phone, floating there like a ghost, unconnected to anything.

Lucas

What's left of my whiskey is rolling around in the bottom of my glass. Goddamn Mercer. Stopped at his trailer. Coupla belts, shot the shit. Tells me his new idea. Gonna fill the tank of his windshield wipers with vodka and run a tube up through the dash so he can flick on his washer and squirt himself all he wants and the cops looking for an open container can go fuck themselves. I told him there's live music up at the resort, let's go. No, he's got some new twitch coming over, a dancer from the titty bar out on the highway. Fuck you, Mercer.

The band sounds good and I turn around to check out the dance floor. Well lookie there, Blondie and some geeze in a Stetson. She got the moves, yes she do. Hello darlin'. Go change your diapers, grandpa, you ain't got a chance tonight. Oh, now he's walking her to her seat, holding her hand up between them like some English fairy. Tips his goddam hat and leaves her all by her lonesome.

The band starts up. I shuffle on over. Evening. This is a real good song, good beat, and you're a helluva dancer.

She takes one look and she's up and rarin' to go. Her hand is small and warm and real soft. I give her a turn, spin, over, hop. My hand slides down her back and around her hip. Give her the lasso, the dirty move, down, up, and down, my hand on her nice soft belly. Spin her around, lean left into a dip, twirl her right and another dip. She likes that. Tornado. Spin cycle. Slide. Slide. Jump rope. Side lean. That's it darlin', over my leg like you're humping it. Let's try that again. Stroll left and stroll right. Our cheeks are close and I feel her heat. The band's working it up to a finish and I reel her in tight. The final note goes WHAM. My arm's around her waist, her face right next to mine. She's got a little sweat on her upper lip like we been bangin' on a hot afternoon.

I ask if she wants a fresh one and she says yeah. I go get us a couple, hand her one and pull a chair up close to her. Lucas, I say.

Krystal.

That's a real pretty name, but not half as pretty as you.

She laughs and pushes aside some of her hair. Ain't twenty, but she ain't bad. She takes a big swallow of her beer like what's next big boy?

They're a good band, I tell her. I'd like to dance with you some more.

She looks down and little dimples come out when she smiles. Yeah, she'd like that too. But first it's off to the ladies. She's up and walking, puts a little extra sway in the caboose just for me.

Out in the truck I got a fifth of Jack near full, the bud I got from that prick over in Riverton, and what's left of the crank. Yes, ma'am, I hope you're ready for a night to remember.

Krystal

I want to dance, okay? Don't make me beg, Terry, for Chrissake, don't make me. Do you even remember what the counselor said? What we're supposed to be doing here? *What you agreed to?*

With him it's rock step, rock step, one, two. Always has been. At least we're out here and dancing. Stop thinking, just go with it. Rock step, rock step.

Lucy's watching. Got her mouth all pinched up, nose crinkled... like we're disgusting. Oh, now she's gonna hide in her book. Used to be Taylor Swift, morning, noon, and night, now it's Greta what's-her-name...Thumb-something...Thumbelina. *Oh my gawd, she's so cooool. She talked at the UN and she's just a kid and she's gonna save the world.* Yeah, well, don't hold your breath.

Now where is he going? Terry, one dance, *are you kidding me?*

No, I'm not mad, I tell him. Yeah, take her up to the room, good idea. Okay, see you back here later. Night-night bunny. I give her a smile and a little wave.

She was about two minutes from a meltdown. What happens when she's fifteen? Ninth grade, tenth? What was I like? "Jagged Little Pill" in my head, sneaking out, smoking pot. Just three years from now. Jesus. We'll make it...right? No good reason we can't.

If he'd just let it go. But no, not Terry. Stomps around the house like he's wearing army boots—*clomp, clomp, clomp.* Gotta let me know, gotta remind me...what I did to him, always what I did to him. *Clomp, clomp, clomp.* Yeah you're mad and yeah it's my fault, all my fault, okay, but you're no angel either.

The old guy standing up at the table over there, with the big white Stetson and a snow-white Hulk Hogan mustache...a bootscooter from way back. Is he coming this way?

All duded up—the hat and leather vest, the bolo tie with a big hunk of turquoise and silver caps on the danglies. Well, yes, I would like to dance.

He escorts me out onto the floor and we flow right into it. Spin and turn and forward and under and reverse and back and under and turn and spin. Knows what he's doing. A firm lead, steady, right on the beat... a partner you can trust, you always know what's coming next. I relax into the music, the singer's voice. We swirl and twirl and glide. The song finishes and we smile at each other, both knowing we're good together.

Another dance? Yes I would.

The band guys fiddle with their amplifiers and sip their beers then count off and start into a Mexican ballad with a nice medium tempo. Dapper Dan leads us into an easy samba and our footwork couldn't be smoother. I love that about dancing, the way the two of you figure out what you can do together and then start moving as one. With some guys it's a battle, a fight every step of the way. But not with this old boy. It's like we've been dancing together for years.

With a light squeeze to my hand, he signals a final turn and a fun little dipsy-do. Looks like he's gonna bust for happy. Walks me to my seat, tip of the hat. Thank you, ma'am, you have a real good night. And he's gone. A real gentleman.

Terry's still not back. Is that him coming in the door? Nope. Where the hell is he? This beer could be colder. If that waitress comes around—

Evening.

Huh? Oh my. Mr. Long and Lean. Rodeo shirt, big silver belt buckle.

He says, you're a helluva dancer.

Grabs my hand and off we go. Doesn't have the old guy's finesse but he's strong, oh, very strong. Fast twirl. Throws me left, swings me around right. Tornado? Been a while. A little show-offy, but he can dance. Letting his hands roam. He likes that side lean. Gives it an extra something that gets me halfway horizontal. Back to that again on the other side. The band's taking it home. How's he gonna finish up? A walk out and a stroll and a low cheek-to-cheek and he wraps me up in his big arms and lays me out real low, and when the music stops his face is right next to mine and he's burning into me with those green eyes. We're breathing like racehorses and he smells like whiskey.

The singer says they're gonna take a break. Walking to the table, I pat my hair back into place.

Well yes, I would like a drink.

Off goes Mr. Slim Hips. Mmm-mmm-mmm. If those jeans were any tighter. He's back with the beers, says his name's Lucas. Fits him head to toe. And he tells me I'm pretty.

Well here we are, aren't we?

He says he'd like to do some more dancing. What he really wants is written all over his face…his very nice looking face with that strong jaw and those green, green eyes.

Miss Dinkybladder says *hey girl*, and I tell Lucas, now don't you go anywhere, I'll be back in a flash. Making my way around the tables everything feels so different. Now I'm at a party I want to be at.

There's one woman in a short pink skirt waiting outside the bathroom so I take my place. I should have brought cigarettes. I'd die for a cigarette. Lucas. Going down into the dip, my hand on his strong back. Mmm. Strong like Vic.

A prune-faced woman comes out of the bathroom and pink skirt goes in. Alone in the hallway now…Vic. Me and Vic.

I'm taking a quick smoke outside the back door at work—Terry would kill me if he knew—and some guy in white pants is up on the ladder next door painting the outside of the Jiffy Lube, sees me looking.

Hey, sweetheart, you got another one of those?

He comes over, him and his big easy smile, and I light him up. Don't you know they'll kill you?

He exhales a cloud and laughs. Least I'll die happy.

Funny guy, Vic. That beaded necklace with a cross on it. Never took it off. Our one night.

Pink skirt comes out, squeezes by me and I wonder where Terry is. And what are we doing, huh? I go in, take the open stall. We're trying to make this family thing work...but he doesn't care, it's all about him, he's off having his little...payback. We come up here, put on a show, and why? He'll be with her next week. I know he will. Damn you, Terry. God damn you.

Out of the stall, I look at my eyes in the mirror. Skin's getting a little thin. In the bar light, Lucas won't even notice. That's funny. I look good when I laugh. Pretty, he said.

I push open the door and start into the hall, but he's right there in front of me blocking the way. I look up at him and he says, out on the highway there's a place you might like, real good for dancing, The Crossroads.

Lucy Ann

What's that noise? Dark. A blast of light and Mom's creeping in from the hallway, hunched over, holding her shoes. She closes the door all careful and it's black again. The clock says 5:11. I smell cigarettes. She's not supposed to smoke. Dad rolls over. He's gonna be so mega pissed. She goes into the bathroom, the lock clicks. A bar of light comes on under the door. The shower starts up. They're gonna fight.

I pull the covers over my head and roll up into a ball, small as I can be. I start to shake and squeeze my arms tight against my chest and try not to think about anything and remember that right before I woke up I was dreaming. There was a big horrible forest fire, roaring into a town like that one in California, Paradise. Everybody running and screaming, driving their cars all crazy trying to escape. Smoke and fire and ashes. Every building burning until there wasn't a single thing left. Stupid greedy adults. Greta blames them, says they're the ones who wrecked everything and it's us kids who are gonna pay. You stole our childhood and you stole our future. How dare you. We'll never forgive you. I will never ever ever forgive you.

Passive

Gillian Reimann

You ride through life like a passenger,
in the front seat
but never the driver,
never the one in control. You want
to be the one in control,
the one who takes charge,
who tears through life with fangs
bared, ripping through
obstacles with bloodstained teeth,
but instead you sit by
offering up your own throat over

                       and over
                  and over again,

while you seethe inside,
snapping at the invisible bars
you erected around yourself.
You prowl and howl within the cage
as your placid smile
cracks a little more each day, waiting,
waiting for the moment you shatter and
break,

releasing the wolf and its slavering
jaws that ache to snap down
and tear through the façade you built,
tear it to shreds so you may finally,
be free.

As I Slept

Geo. Staley

In the early 50s, my mother
        a stay-at-home mom
had one of my baby shoes
and one of my older sister's
bronzed and turned into
        a nearly matching pair of bookends.

My sister's now holds open a door
against the occasional Hawaiian breeze.
Mine keeps in place the grandboy's Dr. Suess books.

This past Monday, as I search for my spare
IN CASE OF EMERGENCY dog tag,
I look, to no avail, in my bronzed shoe bookend.
It's heavy,
        the electro-plated copper still shines,
        the lace frozen in a perfect knot and bow.
The sole has four ¼ inch prongs
that held the adjustable steel bar which,
        when attached to both shoes,
straightened my misaligned feet as I slept.

A year of nightly rigidity worked:
    I walked exactly like all other 21 month olds.

For my parents, the podiatrist, and the culture,
    this was success.
For me, it insured steady feet
    to weather, unknowingly, the strictures of the 50s
    to absorb the free-flowing tumult of the 60s
    and to understand this dichotomy
        for my life beyond.

The Box

Holly Day

We pick it out together, giggle uncontrollably over the pastel lining
the superfluous pillows sewn to the interior, deny
the shadow of cancer and fear that hides in the shadows
in the dark space between our palms when I take your hand.
I call you "Mom" more often now, forgo introducing you by first name
even to strangers. These last days, all I want
is for you to be my mother.

This seems a good enough place to bury your secrets
cushioned in unrealized dreams
of running away. This will be a place
where shouted orders aren't expected to complete you
where cracked pots and conceptual pieces aren't questioned on merit
where bluebirds come gift-wrapped
and sing only of self-preservation.

Backhoes and Bulldozers

Janelle Cordero

The lot of backhoes and bulldozers looks like a sandbox from high up on the freeway, and I remember the yellow dump truck my brother and I played with as kids. It must've weighed fifteen pounds, at least—a foot tall, pure metal construction with real rubber tires. We'd fill the bed up with sticks and rocks and whatever else we could find in the woods. Then we'd push the truck through the dirt, crawling behind it on all fours until we decided to dump the load, dust rising like flour and settling on our hair and skin. And at a jobsite nearby, our dad would be working the levers of a real backhoe, clawing at the ground with the bucket, making his own piles. We'd meet at home for supper, each of us eating our own microwaveable Stouffer's lasagna at the pink kitchen counter while a sitcom played on the 9-inch TV screen, black crescent moons of grime under our fingernails, laugh track punching through the night as we smiled, happy to be done with work, happy to have more of it tomorrow.

LeRoy and Reggie

Darren Montufar

LeRoy was reclined in his armchair when he noticed how pronounced the shadows cast on the wall from the flickering television had become. On the set, cartoon elves poured milk onto a bowl of cereal, creating *Snap, Crackle, and Pop* sounds. Yawning, he looked out the window, where he saw the dwindling gray daylight, what was left of the November leaves on the trees. It would be dark soon. Soon, it would be 1992, which meant LeRoy would be entering his late 30s. Though, with his thinning hair and aching limbs that often made their own snap, crackle, and pop sounds, he felt like he may as well be turning 50.

His son made a slight noise from his spot on the floor, and LeRoy looked back at the television. Another commercial played—this one for the circus that had come to town. *Three nights only!* the voice from the set exclaimed. On the screen, trapeze artists sailed. Clowns spilled out of a tiny car. Audience members held expressions of awe. Lying on his stomach, the boy *oohed* and *aahed* in his small way. It was the affirmation LeRoy had been awaiting.

"Hey, pal," LeRoy said, "I've got a surprise for us."

Reggie kept his face toward the television, his head propped by his hands as he took his time. "What?"

"I got us tickets to the circus. The same one from that commercial."

"When?"

"The tickets are for tonight. It starts in a couple of hours."

"I'm not going."

"What do you mean?" LeRoy brought the recliner up and got to his feet.

"I don't wanna go to the circus."

LeRoy stepped in front of Reggie, blocking the television. "But you love the circus, the people shooting out of a cannon, the high-wire act. The fire-breathing man will be there. We'll get hot dogs and popcorn. I got these tickets for us at a special price through the shop."

"I don't wanna go."

LeRoy stood there looking down at Reggie, who moved his head so he could look between his dad's legs at the television. LeRoy brought his head up and looked out the window. It was darker out now, and the leaves on the trees appeared colorless.

"Well, I have to run these back to Bernard at the shop so he and his boy can go when he finishes his shift. I got them for us because I knew you liked the circus."

"I don't like the circus."

"You have to come with me to the shop so I can take these back. If your mom somehow found out I drove off and left you home alone, she'd go into convulsions."

"Do I have to?"

"It'll be quick. Maybe some people will have Christmas lights up we can look at."

LeRoy and Reggie drove the back roads to the shop where LeRoy worked, allowing them to see some houses and avoid the noise of the main streets. The houses along the way were all like LeRoy's: single story, a single shape, and a single tone of either gray or blue in the waning light. None of them displayed Christmas lights.

At the shop, Reggie sat in the passenger seat as the car idled, his dad inside. He found an invoice in his dad's glove box and folded it into an airplane. With his hands and an exacting eye for precision, he sailed his plane along the contours of the cloth seat and within mere millimeters of the roof of the small car, putting on an uncanny display of aeronautic maneuvering (complete with stunning barrel rolls and somersaults) the likes of which may never be seen again. Any other pilot would have lost his head or surely gone down in flames of valor. Making propeller sounds, Reggie cranked the window down and pretended he was embarking out into the great unknown. He would send letters and give interviews when time permitted, assuming the mission's success, and he let the airplane fly from his hand, sending it through the equitable sky and toward an elusive glint of twilight at the far corner of the parking lot. Skittering onto the pavement, the plane landed with expert control and cooled its jets. Let the celebrati—

LeRoy climbed back into the car, closing the door.

"Bernard had already gone home. I couldn't sell the tickets back." He buckled his seat belt and adjusted the mirror before exhaling loudly from his nose and sitting for a moment in silent thought. "Roll up the window, pal. You're gonna catch a cold."

Reggie cranked the window as the car backed out of the parking lot.

Back on the road, they took a different route, the sky around them now completely dark.

"There aren't any Christmas decorations up." Reggie's head was leaning against the window, his right cheek pressed into the door.

"Maybe it's just a bit early yet, pal. Maybe when we get together in a couple weeks, we can go for a drive and see Christmas lights then. What do you say?"

"Are you going to put up Christmas lights this year? You didn't put any up last year."

"Of course, I'm going to." LeRoy looked over at his son. "Hey, sit up straight. If we get into a wreck, your head will pop off."

Reggie straightened up and kept his head turned toward the window.

A dog could be heard barking somewhere as they drove. The houses on this route were all like the houses they saw on the way to the shop. Many had their lights on inside, some with their curtains pulled open, their interior scenes on full and bright display. In one house, LeRoy could see a family sitting together on a couch as they watched television. In another, he could see a family gathered around a table.

"Mom said I should say 'sorry' about losing the football you gave me."

"You lost the football?"

"A bigger kid at school took it, and then he said he lost it. Mom said I should say 'sorry.'"

"The football cost money, you know."

"It's okay, Gary has more at his house."

LeRoy steered the wheel with both hands at the top, clenching them. To avoid saying anything out of anger, he sat quietly. He thought about what it must be like to be a kid. Nothing that much mattered to a kid. They were so careless with things. He remembered when he was a kid, he'd promised himself he would never forget what it was like to think like a kid—so that if his adult self were ever angry with his future kids, he'd be able to stop and think, *I remember what it was like to be that age, to think like that* and then be able to relate instantly. But now it seemed the most impossible thing to imagine that he'd ever thought like a kid or would ever be able to again.

"I lost things my dad gave me, too. It happens, pal, don't worry about it. I love you—you know?"

Reggie was silent.

After a moment, LeRoy looked over, goading his son.

"You know, pal? I love you."

"I know."

A hurt set into LeRoy then as silence reestablished. He didn't know what other language to speak; all he knew was the one he knew. He bought the boy a football because boys like football, but now it was gone. He knew Reggie liked the circus, but on this night, for reasons unknown, Reggie didn't. The six dollars for the football wasn't what mattered, or the twenty-five dollars for the circus tickets—that was only thirty-one dollars in the long run. Not so much. What mattered were the moments of bonding LeRoy had hoped to secure through those gifts that would now never be actualized, the moments he thought they'd reflect on years later that have no price tag. But Reggie was just a little kid after all; could he fathom something so complex, LeRoy wondered?

"I'm hungry. Can we go make macaroni?"

"Hey, I know what we'll do. Let's do something fun." LeRoy said, now holding the wheel with one hand. "You know what we should do?"

"What?"

Soon, LeRoy and Reggie were seated at a large corner booth at the partly busy burger restaurant LeRoy had driven them to. The plush, curved booth could easily fit six or seven people, and when Reggie sat down, he'd scooched far enough away from his dad as though to allow that many extra guests to join. Their corner booth was at the meeting place of two walls of windows, so both LeRoy and Reggie had windows behind them.

They both slurped from glasses of cola and ice, using straws to drink. LeRoy had just asked Reggie how the spelling quiz had gone. What quiz? Reggie responded. LeRoy said the quiz that had been coming up that we'd studied for last time. Reggie slurped his cola, and then a short time later, he slurped from the straw again and watched the headlights of cars driving along the road outside the window behind his dad, driving off somewhere.

"Here you go, guys!" said the young woman who brought them their plates of hamburgers and fries. "Two burgers and fries for you, no onion, no tomato. Is there anything else I can bring for you?"

"Ketchup!" said Reggie, smile beaming.

"Right here, cutie," the young woman said, pointing to the glass bottle of ketchup hidden behind the napkin holder.

Unphased, Reggie commenced inserting crinkle fries into his mouth.

"That'll be all for now. Thank you, Miss," LeRoy said to the woman.

The two smiled at one another, and the young woman walked away and toward the kitchen. LeRoy continued to watch her as the distance between them grew.

"Do you like her?" Reggie said with a mouth of fries, reaching for the glass ketchup bottle.

LeRoy shook his head and looked toward his son. "No, pal, I don't like her. I don't know her." As Reggie worked on opening the ketchup bottle, LeRoy looked again toward the kitchen, but seeing that the young woman had gone, looked back at his son.

"When are you going to get a new girlfriend? Mom has a new boyfriend."

LeRoy put two crinkle fries into his mouth, followed by a large bite from his hamburger. He chewed, looking out the window behind his son. After much chewing, he said, "Speaking of your mom, what are you and her doing tomorrow after she picks you up?"

"I don't know," Reggie said as he shook the glass ketchup bottle upside down with both hands above his plate to no effect.

"You don't know?" LeRoy said, watching Reggie shake the ketchup bottle.

"Oh, I know! Gary is taking us up to his cabin at the lake."

"Is that right? Do you like going up to that cabin at the lake?"

"Gary said he's going to teach us ice fishing, and he says there's bobcats up there, too."

"Over my dead body Gary is taking my seven-year-old on any ice before it's even winter out."

"What does that mean, your dead body?" Reggie said, still shaking the bottle, the ketchup still uncompromising.

LeRoy continued watching his son shake the bottle.

"You can't just shake it to get the ketchup. You have to hit the '57' on the back and angle it—like this." LeRoy pantomimed, hitting an imaginary glass ketchup bottle tilted at the perfect angle.

"What is the '57?'"

"Scooch over here—I'll show you the trick."

LeRoy and Reggie scooched a little toward one another, and LeRoy took the ketchup bottle.

"See this little '57' on the back of the bottle? You have to tilt the bottle just so and hit the '57' with your hand." LeRoy demonstrated, shaking ketchup out onto his plate.

"Cool!" the boy said, "Lemme try!"

He took the bottle from his dad and mimicked the motion, nearly emptying the entire bottle of ketchup onto his plate. The two shared a laugh.

"I think you got the hang of it. Let me show you another trick. When you're slurping the cola with your straw, and it sounds like it's all out, stab the straw into the ice cubes a few times—mix it up a bit. You'll get more cola that way." LeRoy demonstrated again, jamming his straw into the ice at the bottom of his glass, then taking a slurp of cola and melted ice water.

"Oh, wow! How come I didn't know that?" Reggie did the same with his straw and slurped, taking a full drink of the cola and water.

"Anything more right now, guys?" The young woman from earlier had returned, and she stood at the end of the booth, her eyes fixed on the ketchup covering Reggie's plate, but she said nothing about it.

"Can I have another drink?" Reggie said to his dad.

"One more cola, please," LeRoy said to the woman, who smiled and returned to the kitchen. LeRoy again watched her walk away, smiling a sad smile, but then his smile faded entirely.

Patting his pants pockets and reaching into his jacket, his hands returned empty each time. He then closed his eyes, massaging the front of his forehead with his fingertips.

"What?" Reggie said.

"I just realized I left my wallet at home. I thought we'd be just out and back when we went to the shop earlier, and I didn't think we'd need it."

"What are we going to do?"

The young woman returned, setting down a full glass of cola and ice for Reggie. LeRoy smiled at her before she turned to leave once more.

"What are we going to do?" Reggie said again before drinking from his cola.

LeRoy looked around the restaurant for any familiar face who might be able to buy their meals as a favor. He didn't recognize anyone.

"We'll just ask the nice lady for some boxes for our burgers and ask if we can use the phone in the kitchen to call your mom so she can bring some money."

"I don't want a box. I'm full."

"It's to take with us for later."

"I don't want any more."

"You hardly ate any of it."

"I don't want it."

"Fine. Forget the boxes. I'll just ask the nice lady to use the phone in the kitchen." LeRoy scooched back to his end of the booth to get out.

"No, stop."

LeRoy stopped and looked back at his son. "What?"

"Why don't we do what they did in that movie we watched the one time? Remember? When they sneaked out of the restaurant?"

"No, that's just the movies. People don't really do that. It's illegal."

"But *we* could do it."

"No, pal. Imagine if your mom found out; she'd *really* have convulsions then. And if the judge found out, then forget it—we'd never see each other again."

"I promise I won't tell Mom. I think it would be fun."

LeRoy hunkered down over the table, leaning toward his son. "Really? You think it would be fun, pal?"

"Yeah!" Reggie whispered conspiratorially before drinking more of his cola.

Having scooched back toward the end of the booth, LeRoy could again see out the windows behind Reggie to where his car was parked on the side street. To reach it, they would have to run across the restaurant floor, out and around most of the building, and then run across a street in the dark. It seemed like a ludicrous idea, something only a kid would consider.

"Okay," LeRoy said, his voice dropping to a hush. Both he and Reggie lowered themselves to the table, made themselves small. "You remember where the car is, right?"

"Yep."

"Alright, let's do it. On the count of three, we make for the door. We run and don't stop until we're in the car. Take one last drink of your cola."

Reggie obliged. "Okay," he whispered after.

"Promise me one thing before we do this, okay, pal?"

"I swear I promise I won't tell Mom."

"No, that's not it. Promise me—promise both of us you'll re-member us doing this together years from now."

"Okay, I promise both of us."

"Okay. Ready? One…two…"

Ode to an Infant's Mouth

Mary Rohrer-Dann

—for Elyse Amalie and after Pablo Neruda

Rosy sea-plant of lip and tongue and gum,
explorer of wooden rattles, chair rims,
plastic teething rings, plush blue rabbits.
Connoisseur of tiny fingers, fists, pearly-toed feet.
Happy nosher of aged cheeks, knuckles, knees.
And books! *Frog and Toad, ¿Eres Mi Mama?*
Winnie the Pooh, Buenos Noches, Luna.
Oh, lovely mouth that sings the world into being,
that seeds nascent English *y Español*
in undulant cadences of coo, click,
burble-bubble, shriek, howl, guttural growl.
What worlds await your novice tongue—
salty, spicy, honeyed, oyster-slippery words.
Chewy, chunky, deliciously stinky words.
Words that give *crystal to the crystal,*
blood to the blood...life to life.

Elegy for a Garden

Trapper Markelz

You are a collection of scattered sayings,
errant thoughts that collect into lines,
a bolt of light that births brothers & daughters,
future dads & capable mothers,
golems of sand & soil that beat the odds.

Count up less than 100 days over a lifetime
& all you have is a penny-activated mutoscope
of fleeting moments, a whirlwind
of passionate seeded adventures, strong

like the first sip of coffee in a Paris garden café,
that slithers down the throat of winding paths
and hidden hedges. We don't even have a pile
of letters anymore. The photographs
only come back due to facial recognition.

All the cheek kisses and smudged lipstick
are parting shots. The moments skid
on the trailing accent of your cursive signature
bending toward the bottom of a lifelong page.

I hope this finds you well, Grandma.
Your tight fist held so many flowers
to your chest. I had been so focused
on myself—I missed the years
that added to your creases.

I follow the lines of my own face and neck now
looking for an echo of your inheritance.
I still have the letters you sent me at college.
I miss your fingers—the ones
that once traced letters on my back.

A Poem for Sakambari

—after Jane Hirshfield

Vivek Sharma

Outside the window:
a shower of white and orange—
falling from the branches of heaven
in a vortex, before Indra's
watchful eyes.

Fresh bloom of the night   now falling   in clumps:
The tree feels lighter;   its heart, heavier—

with every fall, there's a promise
the slender tree knows how to keep.

To bloom is to fall...

as you enter the asylum and are left
     daydreaming in the hospital garden with
          irises full of air and life

swinging in Indra's arrogance,
     green stubbornness breaking
like lustful dreams of a war hero, now returning

in the morning
while the courtyard is covered
with heaven's white offering

—just where   the road   bends—

and in my mind, the image of Sakambari:
a trail of smoke pluming upwards
from a cigarette resting in an ashtray.

Curious, child-like eyes
from within the bifocals, and they become
a pair of parijat flowers,
slowly unfurling their petals at night

and swirling into an oblivion
at dawn's first arrival—

while my body breaks
        into blossoms.

For Bill

Joshua Kulseth

I remember most his arms, naturally
brown and strong from work, draped heavy on
the church pew where we sat as a family.
He would tap with his fingertips on
my slender shoulder—little more than
A wisp of flesh—nothing in resemblance
to the looming presence of a man
who molders now in the observance
of no one. Afterwards we were trained to say
of the dead, *they're still in our lives,*
still watching over us. In one way I know
he's still around. A strong arm survives,
pleasant and oppressive like rain: overcast
mornings around warm indoors and sober books.
He taps, a hard rapping of the past,
an incomprehensible hope—strange looks
from family friends who see my beard
grown out and mistake me for the long dead man.
the resemblance *is* striking, weird;
he taps, afraid to be forgotten.

Sonnet for Post-divorce Photosynthesis

Riley Danvers

Late September mists cloak me in shrouds
of diamond dewdrops. Woods are quiet
with listening, still waiting out the   th r e at
as it makes its way through the underbrush.
Not all da   n   gers are clearly visible.
But y o u are.
And the mist transforms me into a silhouette.
I like blending in.
I watch y o u traverse the undergrowth,
searching, scanning, h u   n t i n g.
        I am the hex, a
destiny of darkness waiting in shadow.
        I am magic.   I am memory.   I am
malice un do ing the h a t r e d of your helix.

Trade Wood

Nickolai Vasilieff

Back when Oregon was a mecca of logging, along with good pay and hard living, came the inevitable danger of working hands-on with one-hundred-foot tall, six-foot diameter Douglas Fir and heavy equipment. For every man that perished on the logging runs, a widow and family were left to fend for themselves. Family took some in; others, young, pretty widows, found husbands easily, but many, with less market-able attributes, found themselves alone, barely able to provide food, let alone other basic needs for their young family. Tradition kept these widows out of most gathering places, where they might meet eligible men (church the exception), and over time a new tradition known as Trade Wood began. Barter is as old as humanity, as is the oldest pro-fession, but no self-respecting widow considered such a profession. Barter, on the other hand, had its attraction. With the community of widows growing yearly across the Northern Cascades and Coast Range, men quickly found that firewood was a needed commodity, as was the payment that followed.

Communities frowned on promiscuity but knew that the risk of serious illness, starvation, and death came with long, cold, wet win-ters. A practical yet discreet solution was welcome by all. One can imagine the tradition starting with a shy young man approaching a young widow who shared his feeling of attraction. He couldn't ap-proach a home with a wagon load of wood, so instead, he carried a small bundle of wood kindling, smelling of fir pitch, ready to combust at the strike of a match. Equally shy, the young widow may have been perplexed at first, but no doubt, in time, they struck a bargain. The young man, proud of his achievement, shared his creativity at the local watering hole, and like wildfire spurred on by pitch-soaked kindling, the word spread. Soon, the practice became a tradition to benefit all who participated.

As the mourning spread, so did the creativity. Trade Wood expanded to Trade Food, Trade Labor, and sometimes, Trade Matrimony. But, as with all traditions, when the cause ceases, so does the effect. In the nineteen sixties and seventies, the logging industry declined. New logging practices, innovations, and regulations drowned an industry in decline. Although this tradition may remain in some rural areas, Trade Wood activity likely died as logging and fatalities declined, and the widow population mostly disappeared. Today, one might see a young man carrying a hand full of kindling and notice the heavy kerosene aroma of fir pitch on a special occasion, but it is apt to be a gift of friendship or camaraderie rather than a life-saving jester of mutual benefit.

At the Coastal Commission Hearing on the Desalinization Plant

Kimberly Nunes

The question was water, how to bring more to our lives.
It may all come down to the Western Snowy Plover.
City seats and valley farms, ecologists, and native tribes—
the thing is water, how to bring it to our lives.
Ohlone Esselen Monterey coast, here, where this bird thrives,
the size of a sparrow, the chorus cried—*the ocean is our mother.*
But the question's water—how to bring more to our lives.
It may all depend on the Western Snowy Plover.

Memento Mori

Vanport, Oregon (1948)

Linda Drach

That Memorial Day was sunny. Ned was fishing
or at the tavern in a huddle of toasting Vets.
I sprawled across our blue davenport, smoking
and fanning myself with a Life Magazine.
I was pregnant and all I wanted to do was stare
out the window, swollen feet propped up
in ratty slip-on espadrilles. Sullen. Distracted.
Waiting for something to happen.

From my house on the hill, I had a perfect view
into the bowl of the city, the one built quick
for the farm girls and divorcees
who came from Somewhere, USA to pound rivets.
I worked with them, and liked them—we were all noble
for a minute, but the war was over now. The ones who still
lived down there had nowhere else to go. Afterwards,
I thought maybe the hot plates and matchstick walls
were some kind of blessing. Ten thousand units,
but only a handful at home that day. The rest were out,
looking for something better.

Men in suits arrived in droves, and still,
I didn't understand. I watched them lead hundreds
of horses from the adjacent racetrack. I thought
maybe a parade. Hours later, the dikes broke,
and the wall of water hit the city, yanking down
the windows and walls and rooftops and even
the radio tower, which sailed down the river
and out to sea, to be found later by a ship we built.
I was on my fat feet, belly pressed against the glass,
when a lesser flood soaked my ankles. For hours,
I thrashed in my bloody debris, screaming prayers
to the god of second chances, as everything in me
washed away.

Dad Jokes

Joshua Kulseth

You'll understand when you've lost a parent
how easy jokes come: firing from the hip
the first careless thought that slips
into words (that wasn't meant

to shock, but like breathing, just to exhale).
Death becomes funnier
after the fact, when sifting for
something not broken becomes so stale

and heartbreaking, you need some lightness,
like an under-glare through the cracks
of a doorframe inside some dark
room. It comes naturally, this

morbidity, after so many
years of practice. Maybe its avoidance,
or that old violence
I used to spew when any-

one mentioned his name. Maybe
it's my attempt to cut down the macho

garbage he always threw
in my face,

and how it seems more of a relief now
that he's gone, and we can all stop taking
damage, or being
disappointed how

his insecurities robbed us all
of a father, husband, mentor,
example to strive for—
and who died not knowing us at all.

Or it could just be a really good
joke: an inside joke, and the only one
where it's better being on
the outside.

Jasper

Carolina Atkins

The anger was a pit in the earth, and I finally fell inside. Does Jake know that my mother is dead? He was only five when it happened—when the barn burned down with her in it, and afterwards no one could figure out what went wrong. How could Jake know that I—then six years old—had witnessed his father drop the lit stub of a cigarette into the dried grasses of our yard? Jake was not there with me to watch his father turn and flee into the dark swamp, where the cicadas sang of his trespass. But Jake must know his father is a murderer.

And tonight, twenty-five years later, I know that it is finally time to confront the son for the sins of the father. I'm not leaving any supper on the stove tonight. I won't be coming back.

I make my way to his house, down in the holler of the swamp. It lies past the dark waters, hidden from the main footpaths by cypress trees weeping spindly tears of Spanish moss. I've never seen his house, but I pass by it each day, up on the higher road where the ground is dry. Folks buy alligator skins from him, although some say he also hauls firewood. I don't care. It's night, and the neon green of the water lilies is gray as I wade into the shallow waters, moving towards his little island harbored a mile out in the darkness.

I don't know what I'll do when I get there; I don't even know what I'll ask him. I've dreamed about it: I'll knock on his door—walk right in and tell him to face me like a man. I'll climb in through his window, shake him awake in his bed, and hold up a lantern to my face so he has to look close at every crease under my eyes, every glint of the light on their red rims, the shiny white corneas—so close that he can't turn and hide. He has to look at me—look at me—and sit there cold knowing what he's done.

In the murky dark that makes everything appear more distant than it is, after sopping through a mile of muck, I finally see the gold blinking of two small windows. The house holds its ground beside a pine growing out of the sand of the island. In my head all I can hear is the bright colors of my mother's voice, singing to me from a rocking chair in a cool, dark room: *Hush, little baby, don't say a word. Mama's gonna buy you a mockingbird. And if that mockingbird don't sing, mama's gonna buy you a diamond ring.*

A few yards from the house, where I can hear the faint twanging of a banjo over the wind, I come upon a barbed wire fence. I don't have any wire cutters, and I gnash my teeth in the darkness. But a few steps along the fence line reveal a wooden gate which unlatches easily. And then the scream of a bobcat somewhere in the swamp informs me that the wire must be more for protection against a beast than against a man. I pass through the entrance and close the gate behind me, feeling furtively for the knife in my pocket.

Creeping down the dried brush path on the island, I see that the house is a one-room wooden shack, its base half-sunk into the sand, its roof and windowpanes splintered and dusty. The chimney is a patch of shadow. A small wooden lean-to is built on one side of the shack. Through the window shines the bobbing gold shadows of fire. He is playing banjo somewhere inside, just beyond my sight. Over the sound of the wind, I take my fist and pound it against the door.

Inside, the slow, intermittent music stops. Suddenly my arms are alight with the constricted desire to rip the door away from its hinges and throw it over my shoulder. The door grates open, and the first thing I see is a man—Jake—wearing an eyepatch which barely conceals a delta of red scarring where his left eye would have been. His other blue eye looks out at me clearly. My fist, which has raised itself halfway, lowers. Jake holds a machete in one hand. He's a large man, armored in tough work clothes, his face grizzled. The stench of sweat and swamp and cooking meat exudes from him. A kind of exhausted resignation tracks from the lines under his eyes, down to his beard, all the way to his calloused left hand which hangs beside the dusty folds of his trousers.

"Evenin'," he says in a subdued voice. "You in some trouble?"

An eerie feeling descends upon me—that he has been expecting me. I grip wildly at the handle of the knife in my pocket. I could do it now. Twenty-five years. Twenty-five years to gather the bravery to look into his face. I wish he would spit at me. I wish the nauseating light of insanity would spark in his eyes. But first I have to tell him what I came to say.

Jake's right arm lowers the machete. "I've seen you around. Around town. You lost?"

"Yes," my voice says calmly. "I saw the light. In your window."

"Why don't you come on in." Jake makes room for me to step inside. His movements are slow, almost sleepy, as he shuffles farther into the house.

My blood is a hurricane in my skull. A moment later I find myself standing just inside his door, and the door has been shut. The room is small, cramped, dark, dry. In the back left corner the roof slants diagonally over a straw-stuffed mattress on the floor, covered by a single quilt and a single pillow. The quilt is folded back meticulously. Against the right wall is a small wood-burning stove, faced by a straight back chair. The fire is the only source of light, and it sends warm shadows flickering across the room toward a shelf crammed with jars of fruits and vegetables and the meat of hunted game. Beside the shelf is a pile of hunting gear: a skinning knife, rubber wading boots, a rifle, a raccoon trap, waterproof gloves. On the other side of the stove is the door to the lean-to.

The floorboards creak under Jake's feet as he stands over the stove, stirring a small pot of stew, his face lit by the fire like a wood engraving. "Let me fix you somethin' to eat."

"Ah, no—don't put yourself to the trouble."

"No trouble. No trouble at all. Go on and take a chair." He points to the chair sitting before the fire, with the banjo leaning against it. "I got some good fresh coffee right here. What's your name? Where've I seen you before?"

"We haven't met properly," I say, still standing and suddenly cold.

"How's that?" He pushes a tin cup of hot black coffee into my hands. It smells sweet and vaguely of raspberries. He turns to retrieve another tin cup from his shelf of jars, and I move aside to avoid blocking his path.

I continue, "I mean to say…we've never really met. I've seen you around. You a hunter?"

"Yeah. Trapper, mostly. And furniture maker. That's my chair I built." He points to the chair. "It's made of pinewood."

"It's a good chair."

He grins like a little boy. "Thank you. Please, go on and try it out."

Without meaning to, I'm sitting in the chair, draining the coffee, trying to make my slow mouth say what I came to say. "You don't shoot no animals?"

"What's that?"

"You don't shoot animals? With that gun."

"Only ones that attack me. Otherwise ain't much need for it. 'Cept when I sell skins, I should say. Like from bobcats and gators. Maybe that's when I seen you—when I was sellin' skins in town."

"Maybe so."

He hands me a cup of stew, then sits on the floor next to my chair, facing the fire. "Where you headed so late?"

Suddenly the smell of stew is not so appetizing. "I...guess I wasn't headed much of anywhere."

Jake does not reply.

My mother sings in my head. *If that diamond ring turns brass, Mama's gonna buy you a looking glass.* Suddenly a fury awakens in me like a bobcat and tears at the inside of my lungs. I want to strike Jake to the floor and scream, *Did you know? Did you know all this time and never even came to find me?*

Jake looks calmly into the fire.

"You play the banjo?" I hear myself ask in a dry, cracked voice.

As if awaking from a reverie, Jake says, "Some. My father left it to me. Built it with his own hands."

"Your father?"

"Yeah, left me this banjo."

"Where's your father now? He live here with you?"

Jake laughs. "Can't say that he does."

"Your own father don't live with you?"

"Nah. He lives on his own."

"Where's that?"

He grins. "You really wanna know?" The firelight is waving across his face.

"Where is he?"

Jake leans back on the palms of his hands. "When I was a boy, my father used to tell me the story of Jasper the duck. His father, my grandfather, presented him one day with a small, fuzzy white duckling. My father named it Jasper, and raised it up 'til it was a full grown. That duck followed him everywhere. Then one day, my father woke up, leaned over the side of the bed to where Jasper normally slept, and Jasper was nowhere to be found. My father went all over the house, calling, "Jasper, Jasper!" No Jasper. He went all over the yard, calling, "Jasper, Jasper!" No Jasper. He went even further, out into the swamp, callin', "Jasper, Jasper!" No Jasper at all, not even a feather. Finally his Pa said to him, "Well, son, I guess Jasper got caught up by a fox." But just then, my father looked up into the sky and saw a flock of wild geese flying. "Jasper, Jasper!" he cried—and he knew that Jasper must've come across a nice family of geese and decided to join them in their flight, somewhere he could be with others more like himself."

Jake pauses and gives a lopsided smile at the fire. "I always figured my own father was somethin' like Jasper." He chuckles at the end of his story, and falls silent. A log shifts and slides disdainfully in the fire. Outside, the cicadas scream and the wind bumps against the window. The knife hangs heavy in my pocket. Looking down, I realize I have been eating the stew he gave me, and my stomach churns. I look around again at the dingy jars on the shelf, the misshapen hunting gear, the lumps in the mattress. Jake's blue eye glints, still fixed on the fire. The red scarring under his eyepatch reminds me of that old story my grandmother used to tell about the Nile River turning to blood.

I shiver with sick cold. "Can you see with only one eye?"

Jake turns and laughs a little. "Yeah, it ain't a problem. Lost the leftie when I was five, so they tell me. Wanna see?"

"No. Just tell me what happened."

"There was some kind of fire."

My chest hurts. "Some *kind* of fire?"

"Yeah, that's what they say."

"But don't you know what *kind* of fire it was?"

Jake looks at me at last with an unmasked concern in his eye, but I can't control the rising in my voice. He replies, utterly bewildered, "Friend, I can't say I know what you mean. You in some kind of trouble?"

"Stop asking me that!" I rise from the chair, suddenly uncertain what to do with the cup of stew in my hand. "Wasn't this supposed to be your stew?"

"Don't worry," Jake says, standing. "You're my guest, and I reckon I'll finish up the rest later on. Why don't you stay the night? I can point you in the right direction in the morning. You look worn out."

"I only gotta know about the fire."

Jake regards me with a deep trouble in his eye. At last he says, "Alright. But have a seat again. I'll tell you what I know."

Jake is silent for a long moment as he sits on the floor next to my chair. "There was a fire," he begins, "at a neighbor lady's house. A good woman. I think I remember hearing that she was alone in the house. I only have the vaguest memory of it—some kind of heat, and orange, and darkness. It was my mama who always told me the story afterwards, said nobody knew how the fire got started, 'cept it must have been an accident, 'cause there was no one in town who would've done such a thing. She says fire sometimes just starts, and all we can do is put it out. She never really told me how the fire took my eye—said there was no point knowin' all the awful details. I don't remember it at all." Jake pauses and looks out the dark window, listening to the wind. He continues, "I don't know why I would've done it, but the story goes that at five years old, I ran into the fire. They say it was to save that lady, but I'm not so sure. I don't know what I thought I could have done. I dunno...that's all I know about it." He looks at me from the side. "Can I ask...well, what else do you wanna know about it?"

"Your father," I ask, "your father. Didn't you see him?"

Jake's brow wrinkles in confusion. "My father? I can't say...I can't say at all whether my father was there. Best I can remember, I always figured he'd flown away by that time."

I rise in a fever from the chair, pulling my hand out of my pocket where it has been gripping the knife, and reach it out towards Jake.

Ambition

—after Linda Gregg's "Etiology"

Natalie Marino

failure made me   failure
and the iron scent of spilled
blood   the silence
between the steps of   red ants
mine is a field
filled with mistakes
        I have collected the dying
petals of roses   and buried
sacraments in a sea of grass
        I have watched children
pray in the sky's open cathedral
        their hands stained with berries
heaven
is a garden planted in spring

Early Spring, Oregon Coastal Hills

Cecil Morris

A day of mist and drizzle interrupted
by rain, the light damped to evening gray all day.
The crows have disappeared, hiding their black selves
from this weather, this wet and dusky gloom—
the long doom of dripping eaves and sound bundled
off by wind, muffled by rain, the world holding
its breath and waiting. A still life in shades of green
and mud and fawn. A doe and her slender yearling
appeared unmoving, too, their big eyes unblinking,
their ears turned to me, and we watched each other,
patient, still, letting time hesitate between us,
a caesura, a nap. Finally they turned away,
done with me, and started a slow-motion walk
up hill, the doe wide and swaying, gravid, stately,
the yearling a sylph, a slip, a forecast weaving
around the mother's trail.

I Hold My Body Soft

Eva-Maria Sher

I hold my body soft when trouble comes
and seek the company of other mothers
who keep all feathered blessings in their palms,

who offer Truth to those with open arms,
refuse to wail and wait, would rather
hold their bodies soft when trouble comes,

or build a wall of love where others harm,
bind wounds where others blame and dither
and keep all feathered blessings in their palms,

and bless our planet with my healing balms.
Though I've never given birth, I'm still a mother,
I keep my body soft when trouble comes.

Where there's a wall, I'll tear it down,
where one door's blocked, I'll find another.
I keep all feathered blessings in my palms.

Where there is fire, I will sound alarm
and then make certain we support each other
and hold my body soft when trouble comes
and keep all feathered blessings in my palms.

Drinks before Dinner with the Moon's Half Shell

Shelly Krehbiel

Tonight after too much wine too quickly
I stand in the kitchen alone and wonder
if my son would have been tall. And then
I see him, standing in the doorway, all eighteen
or nineteen years of him, telling me about his day,
how he fixed something I hadn't noticed was broken.
He is tall. And, he has blue eyes, dark blue,
not like ice, not like that woman I dated who tasted
like stars, who let me have the sunset view as we stood
on the butte and kissed the dark in. He has sandy hair,
with bits of red in it, like mine or my sister's.
He's wearing a basketball jersey and grinning,
waiting for something I'm making on the stove.

I never wanted to be my mother. Never wanted
to be standing at anyone's stove until I found myself
standing at my own and no one waiting for anything
from me. I could stir and chop my way into something
that fed me, that tasted good, tasted wholly mine.
And now, this vision of the boy I would have named
becoming the man he would have been. Tonight
I would like to be a little more drunk or a little less,

so I walk out on the porch to get some air, to let
the half-moon see me. I don't get to keep him,
but isn't it funny how I can see him so clearly
and never think to imagine what of him looks like
his father, the *he* I've never wanted or dreamed.

And isn't it strange too how he doesn't look anything
like the woman I would have wanted to make him with,
whose brown eyes I wanted my son to have,
who held me and made me imagine I could want
a son at all. She's the one I still dream sometimes,
even though it's been many years since she's gone.
Now when I dream her, I'm telling her to get out
of my house. I stop her from taking what's mine.
Usually it's my cat she tries to carry off, but once
I was keeping her from taking my boy, pushing her
out the door. In the dream he was younger, five or six,
but still his sandy hair, his blue eyes, like mine,
his little arms holding a cat or a basketball. I saved
him and me and the cat. I got to keep all of us.

The Grass

Pattabi Seshadri

It was when I stopped at the railroad crossing,
watching the grass move
behind the light, metal and paint,
blades leaning at me
in the late afternoon, sniffing at me
with a thinking look
in the gasoline-rippled air,

weeds really, bristling
with spiked seed-pods and serrated leaves,
hissing and arcing out of brackish ditches,
raging the field with an abundance
as thick, wide and faceless
as an arctic massif,

trampled aster-fractals
leaching the sharp oil
of cross-country droppings,
dark, deep lace loopings,
protein dispersal technologies
self-made on self-soil,
acting on any beast wandering among them

to feed, to educate, to train,
and lure into the wilderness
with its head cracked open,
spilling reckless profusion;

it was when I watched each blade
bow its seedhead to the ground
until it almost touched
then spring back up
in what seemed at first a dance
but began to repeat
too many times,
as if it was not alive, but a machine,

that I saw how little
I belonged to anything.

To Be Human

Mark Sullivan

"To be human is to be at a dead loss."
—Elizabeth Bowen

Is to walk through the snow that has not yet fallen
and to feel it crystalizing around you out of the air. Is
to know that the past is past and yet see
how your father's face in the photograph has changed
to resemble your own. Is to hear the school band practicing
"Jingle Bells" every day across the street through the windows left
open because of the pandemic, and to realize the off-tune
horns and unsynchronized drums are slowly converging
toward a melody. He was a drunk and so entangled
in unarticulated feelings that whatever escaped to
the surface seemed lost in that lighter element; and he
was kind and kept improvising stories to you as the dark
enclosed everything in its sudden endings. Is to be able
to hold two opposing thoughts in the mind at
the same time, as F. Scott Fitzgerald said, thinking perhaps
of Keats, his heard and unheard melodies. And to watch
pigeons plunge through December air like a descant of notes
across the staves of a score, while the burnt taste
of coffee shadows your mouth. To add all these things

together and to know that still the sum never equals
the number of waves breaking on the cold sands of an inlet.
To remember with longing how the sky would whiten
at four o'clock above those waters at this time of year,
holding the last light in an unbounded suspension,
and to understand that this still occurs without you
to witness, that *nostalgia* is a combination of sickness and
home. And does that mean the sickness and the home
are one? *Can't wanting want what's human?* your wife used to quote
from Elizabeth Bowen, and you never quite knew what she meant
until you read the story about the young lovers endlessly
wandering abandoned war-time London on a winter's night
because they had nowhere to be alone. And then it made sense:
how finally they would wind up at her shared flat, the woman
falling into exhausted dreams, the on-leave soldier lover sitting
up with her flatmate, who asks the unbearable question. How with no
ill-will or wrongdoing all those people end up deadlocked
between dream-life and wakefulness, frustration and desire, none
knowing quite how they arrived there, just that this is now their home.

Payroll Reminder

Cat Dixon

I meant decimals, but my fingers typed decibels
and my email was *Remember: turn those hours
and minutes into decibels on your payroll
spreadsheet. It's due today.* Ten minutes becomes .17
and 55 minutes is .92. I have a cheat sheet pinned
to the corkboard above my desk. I'm not good at math.

If we turn those hours worked into decibels, how will
they be recorded? Ten minutes is the ring of the phone,
the ding of the Ring doorbell's motion detector with
the buzz of the bee on the playback. Perhaps the bee
needed relief from the heat—the garden isn't
as bee-friendly as we thought.

Five minutes is the mail carrier shoving a bouquet
of junk and bills held by a loose rubber band into the mail slot.
More time lost to the urgent emails commanding create this,
edit that, remove this post, send that letter, refund this.
Type. Type. Type. Type. Type. Backspace.

An hour is the meeting that could've been a phone call;
a phone call that could have been an email—an email
that would expand like the universe, bcc'ing every
blackhole, every potential earth; an email that is a crackling list
of everything I must do before 5 p.m. Email after email
dictates with a boom every action for the rest of my life.

The rest of my life is this office where I stand alone
at the standup desk staring at a photo of my son. Here he is
7. Somewhere he is now 19. When I started working
in this office I was in my 20s. Now my hair is gray
and I've ballooned with the emails, bills, and Wix.
There is no vacation, no sabbatical, no rest.

I resend the payroll reminder: *Send me your hours.*
I meant decimals. Tell me how you've spent your life.

The Three to Eleven Shift

Phil Wetjen

The windows had all steamed up again. Between the darkness outside and the wet glass, all they could see through the window was the glow from the bright arc-lights over the lot.

Glenn was sitting on the counter, looking out towards the lot, as though the window was clear. His eyes were focused out where the pumps were, even though he couldn't see them. It was as if he knew, from sitting there in that spot so often, what the view should be—so why should he look away.

David was leaning on the counter next to Glenn. No one had spoken for a while. David looked to his father-in-law, and noticing his stare, got up to wipe the window again. He used the rubber wiper on a stick that we normally used to clean the windshields on the big diesels. He cleared the window carefully, putting the wiper right against the metal frame and bringing it all the way across the window in a straight line, just the way he did it on his own truck. Or on any other trucks that came in, Boyd thought. David drove his own truck all up and down the west coast, and he knew how important a clear windshield was.

Boyd was standing behind the cash register, next to the little electric heater. He was wet and cold, and wished that he could sit down right in front of the heater and try to dry off, the way he had been before Glenn and David had come by. He could probably go ahead and sit down. Glenn had said out loud how wet he was when they came in. But Boyd couldn't sit just yet. He just wasn't sure of Glenn yet. Boyd had only had this job for two months, and even though he'd learned a lot in that time, he was still the kid. He was older than the day man and the guy that alternated with him on the three to eleven shift, but Boyd was the newest on the job, and was still the kid. He knew time would change this, if he kept on learning, and maybe if one of the others left. At least then he'd get a fifth night and a little more money. Meantime, he'd better stay on everybody's good side. He took a side-step closer to the heater.

"Still coming down like before," David said. He was almost down to the bottom frame now. Glenn was watching him wipe. Boyd could tell that Glenn was thinking windshields.

"Now tonight," Glenn spoke up, "and any night, I don't care how hard it's raining, I want you to hose off the windshields on the diesels, and scrub them if they need it. Those fella's spend a lot of money on fuel here, and we want to give 'em good service. Just 'cos it's raining here, it may be dry five miles down the road, and there'll be bugs and grease all over their windshields."

"OK," Boyd said in a low voice. He didn't think he'd do any windshields tonight, though. On a hard rain night like tonight, it was enough just to fill the tanks, and check the oil and tires. And the paperwork besides. It was impossible to keep the papers dry, so he had to run back and forth from the pumps to the office, remembering the figures from the pump to fill out the new forms the state required on all diesel sales. And it was even harder if the drivers paid by check or credit card, like most of them did.

Boyd could see doing the windshields on a summer night when there were on and off showers, but tonight it must be raining hard all the way to San Francisco. That was the problem with Glenn; they could never talk back and forth about the truck stop, or anything else. It was always Glenn talking and Boyd saying OK.

A car was approaching. They all watched it. It went through the stop sign and disappeared behind the café. The car was either going through, or stopping at their little restaurant, across the lot. The upper part of David's window was beginning to steam up again.

The car reappeared on the other side of the café, and the lights turned toward them. Boyd knew then that it was coming in. He put on his ball cap and picked up his raincoat. After he sidled past Glenn, he put on his raincoat as he walked to the door. The car had just stopped in front of the forward pumps as Boyd opened the door.

When he stepped outside, Boyd felt glad to be clear of Glenn and David. It was still cold out, but it felt good to move again. If he kept moving, he felt warmer, even though he got wetter, and froze when he stopped.

The driver only wanted twenty dollars of Regular. Boyd stayed down by the rear bumper while he watched the pump click off the gallons. He felt water go down his neck. He had been thinking about getting a new hat after the last few nights. A cowboy hat—a Stetson. After having rain drip down his neck, he knew why so many of the drivers wore them. And cowboys too, he guessed.

After he replaced the gas cap and nozzle, he came around the car to take the money. He hoped for a twenty-dollar bill, so he wouldn't have to run back in for change. It was not a twenty, but two tens—just as good. He took them and turned back.

As he walked in, he knew that Glenn had been talking about him, and thinking of work for him to do. Boyd didn't understand why he had to be kept busy every single minute of the shift. Why did they feel they were losing money if he wasn't doing some busy work? He didn't even get time off to eat during the shift. He had to eat in between customers, which sometimes meant not at all.

Glenn began telling him that there were more oil containers to be filled, and to be sure to get the restrooms mopped up. David had to add that the odd lumber in the big shed still needed to be stacked.

Boyd was glad that they had thought of nothing big tonight. Actually, he was lucky that Glenn was here. David usually thought of bigger things, like wanting his truck washed and scrubbed. The worst, though, was Glenn's wife, who tried to run the café. When she was around, Boyd usually spent every spare minute cleaning up the lot. Glenn's daughter, David's wife, was the best. She needed help with stuff sometimes, but she never came up with busy work. Boyd could even talk to her a bit, about business stuff.

There was no more reason for Glenn and David to stay, now that they had given him his chores. Boyd wished they'd just get out of here and leave him alone. He would take care of all the cars and trucks that came in. Why couldn't he just sit by the heater and listen to the game.

Boyd looked over at his lunch behind Glenn. Sarah had made him soup again. Boyd tried to remember what kind. He could see her at home, pouring it this noon. Tomato, he thought. God, that would be good. Hot soup, and sit by the heater. Of course cars would come in for gas as soon as he sat down, but that was part of the job. At least he'd be alone in here.

Finally, Glenn stood up to leave. *He must have a hot meal at home too*, Boyd thought. Before Glenn would leave, Boyd knew he'd have to be told to make sure he got everything locked up right at the end of the shift.

Later on, after nine o'clock had passed, Boyd felt better. He'd managed to eat dinner with only two interruptions, both cars. That was the main problem with this place, he thought. You just couldn't serve both cars and trucks at the same station. Not with just one guy on duty, anyway. They just took away from each other. Either the cars interrupted the diesel routine of fuel, oil check, windshield and tire check, or the trucks kept him so busy he never even saw the cars. Eight pumps were just too much for one man.

Boyd thought a lot about working at a regular gas station, with only cars to take care of. He'd be pretty good at it, since it'd be so much easier than this place. There was also a new truck stop north of town, which only took diesels, and had four pump jockeys and a separate cashier. And there, all the pumps were covered. That was really important this time of year.

Boyd tried to imagine summer here at this stop, and cleaning windshields in a summer rain like Glenn had said. Somehow Boyd didn't think he'd be here for that. Summers it was just too easy to get jobs picking things. Summer was the time for an outside job, not now in this endless rain.

Boyd remembered one summer, two or three years ago, when Sarah had gone out to pick with him almost every day. They worked the strawberry crop in June all the way through beans and peas to the apples in October, and even a few days of walnuts and filberts after the rains came. All that, and they had never had to go more than twenty miles from home.

Talking with the other pickers, Boyd heard that if you traveled to the harvests, you could work just about all year round. You'd stay on the west coast, just following the crops, from lettuce in Arizona all the way up to apples in Washington, and even wheat in eastern

Washington, if you were good with machinery and knew where to go.

Boyd was going to do that someday, maybe this year, now that he'd just about had it with the truck stop, and jobs like it. He'd mentioned it to Sarah a while back, but she'd said he wasn't quite ready for that yet. Especially that he'd be riding trains in between harvests. But he felt ready this time. Maybe this year, after the summer of picking around home, he'd just join the men, and keep on picking. He could mail money home, and come home every once in a while, sort of for vacations.

Yes, he'd bring the idea up again tonight. He'd sure miss Sarah if he ever left, though. If he was cold and wet like this and somewhere down in California, he'd have no one to turn up the heat when he got home, and no one to put out hot tea and make him a sandwich, and turn on the shower while he got undressed, so he'd be warmer sooner.

All this made him think of home tonight, and he looked over at the clock to see how long he had. Ten minutes of ten. Another ten minutes and he'd start the closing chores. First the bathrooms in the café, then closing the bay doors, then locking the shed, and then, at twenty to eleven, starting to count the money and take readings from the pump meters. All this went much easier if no cars or trucks came in. Maybe the bad weather would keep them away tonight. Sometimes, before doing the money or the pumps, Boyd would turn off the big arc lights over the lot. On a night like tonight, you couldn't see the station from the highway without the lights, so that would keep most people from coming in, unless they were regulars or locals and knew the station was here. Boyd thought he would do the lights early tonight, even though he knew Glenn wouldn't like it.

The whole thing was, he only got paid till eleven, and if he kept the station open and the pumps on till eleven, he'd never get out till eleven-thirty. And anyway, then girls and the cook couldn't leave until he did, and they'd be angry if he didn't get things done soon after eleven, so Glenn could just put up with it if he found out.

At ten twenty-five, after the bathrooms and shed were done, and before the money and pumps, a big car and trailer rolled in. At least it's not a truck, Boyd thought. He'd get this car started and then turn off the lights.

The car was a big old Chrysler Imperial. Yellow. About a '66, Boyd thought. It was in perfect shape. The trailer was pretty big for a car—about a twenty-five-footer.

A man stepped out on the passenger side and asked Boyd to fill it up. Boyd had to struggle for a moment to get the nozzle behind the license plate and into the filler pipe, because the trailer hitch was in the way. He managed that and stood up as the other man got out of the car. This man was much older, about seventy, while the passenger side man looked in his fifties.

The older man stepped away from the car and looked around, mainly at the station. Boyd knew he was looking for the restrooms. When the man turned to him, Boyd told him they were over in the café. The man nodded and walked slowly around the trailer.

The other man, meantime, had circled the rig the other way, around the car, and come up to Boyd.

"Where are we, exactly?" he said, laughing a bit.

Boyd understood his confusion. The highway ran four miles east of town, and at night, if you weren't watching the signs too well, you might not realize where you were. Some cars actually drove right by the exit to the town, even though they wanted to go there. They'd pull in, totally bewildered, not sure if they had gone too far, or not far enough.

Boyd explained where the station was located, and asked which way they were heading.

"We're going down to Sacramento," he said. "From Tacoma."

He seemed eager to talk.

"I'm riding home with my dad. He's been with us, living in his trailer there, for a few months, and now he's going back. He wanted to go on his own, but I figured, you know, that a lot of things could happen on the road in winter, so I figured I'd better come along. Just in case. Had to take time off work".

"Oh," Boyd said. They just stood there a moment, looking at the cement pavement. Since the man didn't move away, Boyd added, "that's his car, then."

"Yes, beautiful, isn't it? A real pimp car." He laughed.

Boyd laughed too, but he didn't know how it was funny. He'd have to ask Sarah about this tonight. The man seemed nice otherwise. Why did he use that word?

"It must be worth a fortune now, and it's running perfect. Probably last forever, especially with him driving it. He treats it better than he treated me."

Boyd thought that was funny. At that moment, the pump shut off, the older man reappeared, and the son moved off to use the restroom.

Boyd topped off the tank. The older man seemed shy. He was pulling at the water hose, seeing if it worked. Water poured out and he looked over at Boyd.

"This is good water for drinking, isn't it?"

"Yes sir" Boyd said.

The older man nodded and pulled the hose to the trailer's tank and began filling it. After a moment the son returned and paid the bill. He walked with Boyd to the office.

"We must be about halfway now, don't you think?" he said. Boyd had to think a moment. He was used to figuring distances from Portland.

"Yes, I guess so," he said.

"How are the passes down south?" the man asked.

"OK, the last I heard, but let me get started closing up and I'll call the state road report again."

"Thanks. Looks like the old man's gonna be pumping water for a little while yet."

The son went out. His father hadn't moved from his spot by the trailer. The son circled the rig, looking over the tires as he went.

Boyd watched them as he turned off the lights and pumps and flipped the sign around so "Sorry Closed" faced outside. He was now done except for the money. While he waited on the phone to get through to the road report, he saw the father capping the water tank and feeding the hose back into the spool. The son was in front of the car, looking at the grill or the headlights.

It was funny how they acted. They seemed to be enjoying their trip in spite of themselves. The son had talked of the trip like it was a chore, but he acted like he was enjoying it. And the old man, for all his quietness, still seemed quite content. Boyd thought he resented his son having to be there, but liked him there anyway. They weren't talking much—Boyd hadn't seen them speak at all, but they were enjoying each other and the trip. They'd probably have great memories of it, and talk about it and look back on it a lot.

Sarah always said things were that way. That even the bad times were good. That the bad times were even better than the good in the long run. Boyd knew that summer of picking with Sarah had an awful lot of sore knees and cut fingers, but he never thought of that now. From here at the truck stop, that summer couldn't have been better. Maybe in a summer or two, the rainy nights at the truck stop might seem cozy and happy, instead of cold and wet like he felt now. And he'd have memories of people like this father and son. This wouldn't be a bad memory at all.

Boyd ran outside.

"Passes are clear of snow, but possible icy patches," he called. The son was standing by the car, with the door open. He waved and yelled a thank you. The father, in the driver's seat with the window open, nodded. The son got in and they pulled out.

Boyd ran in to count the money. He thought he might make it home by eleven-fifteen if he hurried. He was looking forward to getting home, getting warm, and telling Sarah about the father and son while he ate some dinner.

Turns My Head Around

Steven Mayer & Linda Fuss

Sleep is better as my rested body rises early to breathe, stretch into a
new day, and shower while humming a few old songs. My mate lingers

asleep in bed. She is motionless, dreaming deeply, a smile on her face.
A gentle kiss arouses. Before I depart, our daughter calls

full of questions, if life is good at our end. Her questions wonder if we
are happy, healthy, active. Unthinkingly, I mention

things I've done: dishwasher unloaded, clothes washer started, flower
vases refreshed, sweet peas newly cut. Our daughter is quiet. Later, my
mate questions

my bragging tone. I explain my comments comfort our daughter far
away that her mother is cared for—no more, no less. My mate nods

her smile sweeps bad vibes away. She suggests it may be better for *her*
to mention the things I've done. I walk

the beach slowly with hard wind in my face and without the glimmer
of sunshine, finding my way to a coffeehouse. I linger

longer, ponder my mate's comment. It turns my head around. When our daughter calls on another day, I avoid

mention of the things I've done. I share what her mother has done to make me happy and in love with her. Our daughter gleefully listens

discloses what I have done to make her mother happy.

Tikkun Olam

Suzy Harris

A whole tiny world lives
within its swinging doors,
doors with tiny hinges,

one hinge askew,
closed up with a rubber band
for months now,

moved from bookshelf
to kitchen counter
to windowsill, simply

asking for a bit of glue,
a tiny hinge.
To watch my beloved

rescue the *retablo*
with a new tiny hinge
is to fall in love all over again.

Sonnet for Post-divorce Photosynthesis

Riley Danvers

This will never be about y o u.
Birdsong dances in August sunlight.
Somewhere a campfire splits open the air,
fills nostrils with crackling smoke.
Nothing moves. Or is everything   always
moving?   Nothing placates a   w o u n d e d
heart like the towering peace of forest echoes.
Daylight bombards the canopy, explodes
the understory into emerald, sage, and pine until even
the soil glows with shamrock. This is why
I clothe myself in bigleaf magnolia,
stars of the forest pulsating
with whispered oscillations of stomata.
This will always be about y o u.

Crossing the Bourne Bridge

Cape Cod, Massachusetts

Ellen Sazzman

ghosts slip in and I understand the meaning of unbidden.
I keep driving east to Coast Guard Beach,

eroding precipitously, but the shore spreads as if to fill
the vacuum left by those no longer.

Waves knock me to my knees where I study the sand for
fossils of abraded histories.

Who can write on water or slice it with a pen's knife? Nothing
imprints on this breaking expanse

but one can walk far enough to shape a silhouette of absence
on the horizon, mane of snow-blown surf

molded to earth's neck, ancient seabirds curving into a fog
thick with risen questions. Once

friends swam in the ocean and children flew diamond kites.
Today seals and sharks congregate. There is

never only the once. Whenever my sons return, there is always
the tide swallowing shoes, stones, skeletons.

I will hug my sons, hand them the string, and instruct them to run,
kite lifting, shadows splintering—now Untether

She Is Plant and Animal

Maya Muir

Roots
stumble slowly, numbly, hold fast.
Dailiness of love's dumb chores
hardly deserves words.
She hears the child call in the night,
sleeps to the man's back beneath the quilt,
warm as honey, as blood.
Eyeless topography the tendrils know,
filaments fine and thready,
pale and greedy,
sucking mineral satisfactions, liquid flow,
binding, binding to the here, the now.

Anchored,
roots shoot her trunk's arrow
to climb the sky
tuning to angles of light.
Star's sugar spins along her veins
as branches curl to claim the warmth,
scent of fir and cedar.

She Is Plant and Animal

The rolling pageant of days, spring and fall,
thimbles of gain and loss,
rings blossoming slowly in the heartwood.

Startled,
then, she hears the wind's keen invitation
to the blooddance. She remembers
she is animal
as well as plant,
would answer the call,
would go,
if she could rip the webbed roots,
the small child's furious grasp.
She would—on all fours—
        race after that burning moon.

The Flavor of the Sea

Holly Day

I bare only half of my history to you, spreads my hands wide
to hide the stories that should stay buried. There are screams
sandwiched between pages of sunlight, blood washed into wasted
>   breath
parts of me that will always be stained with dirty fingerprints
will never wash clean.

I set my pleasant thoughts carefully on the quilt before you, delicate
>   as china
let them unfold into bright, floppy paper flowers fancy enough
for displaying, half-opened, in jacket pockets at formal functions.
I can be good and pure for you, I can,
I will ignore the whispers like needles
the panicked dreams of escape.

A Death in Curry County

Shawn Schenck

The house was sterile, smelling of stale bleach and cigarette smoke. No matter how hard he scrubbed or sprayed, there was no removing that smell. It was in the carpet, deep within the pores of the drywall, and left the popcorn ceiling a soft shade of brown. He pushed the front door open, inhaling the cold, clear breeze, and listened for the soft *clack* as it closed behind him, the same sound he'd heard a thousand times before. The sky was overcast, painted in thick strokes of cloudy gray.

The driveway seemed smaller despite the same green Escort sitting in its space. For the first time, Benji noticed how faded it had become. Despite his memories of the car, it had never been shiny and new. It was a hand-me-down through and through, handed to his mother for the asking price and handed to him when she no longer left the house. He could still remember how excited she was to pick him up from school the day she bought it. There'd only been a few times in his life he'd seen her so happy. She'd been happier then than when he brought home his freshman report card a few years later. He'd been so proud of himself, of the four A's printed beside each course on that off-yellow sheet. She glanced at it with the same empty look she gave to junk mail and credit card offers. Benji imitated her unimpressed look as he studied the car.

Benji closed in on it, reaching for the worn-out handle on the driver-side door. The cigarette smell was worse than inside the house, warring with the handful of felt trees hanging from the rearview mirror. Some smells don't go away, and some stains can't be cleaned. Or maybe that was how it'd always been, stained and stinking, without the shine or sheen one imagined when remembering or dreaming. In that moment, it didn't matter.

Rain pounded the roof of the Escort like marbles on a wood staircase. The windshield wipers swept back and forth, fighting off a deluge of disorienting streams, only briefly revealing the flash of yellow lines. Benji followed the cosmic glow of tail lights that blossomed and burst through his watery gaze. When the rain was at its worst, just before the wipers washed it away and temporarily cleared his vision, he was sure he knew how it would feel to slowly sink to the bottom of the ocean.

Down, down, down. The car displacing the water and slipping into darkness.

Down, down, down. The muted whisper of pressure pushing in around him—pressure like the weight of the world.

Then the wipers fluttered and cleared his view, and he was back on the road.

A white blur grew before him, and he swung the Escort toward it, parking near the unfocused facade of the old building. A woodgrain plaque hung beside the twin doors with the words *Redwood Memorial Chapel* pushing out in a low-contrast, washed-out gray. He saw it in brief, fleeting flashes of clarity as the wipers swiped away the rain. It felt fitting. His memories were all gray, washed out, and faded. Faded but not forgotten. And when he looked back on them—really looked—they stood out amongst the grain in brief, fleeting flashes.

Benji watched the sign disappear and reappear through the rain. A dull thud throbbed through his left hand. His fingers were wrapped around the door handle, the knuckles pulled tight and losing color. He'd been fine all morning and hadn't cried in a few days.

He glanced around the car and spotted his sweater balled up in the passenger seat. He remembered finding it at Secondhand Surplus, the thrift store he and his mother had frequented. Slipping his fingers between the hangers on the rack, his face lit up at the sight of the familiar image: the bold, white lettering spelling out *Suspiria* in a disorienting wave. He'd begged and pleaded for her to buy it, to accept that he'd seen the movie and loved it. She feigned moral opposition, unwilling to admit that she couldn't afford it. The sweater hung from the rack all year, and with every visit, he'd plead and beg her to buy it. His pleading and begging had paid off, and he lit up after reaching into the snowflake gift bag that Christmas.

He stared at the sweater and remembered meeting Tara, walking home from school that October day. He had been too embarrassed to introduce himself.

"I love that movie," Tara said. She stood tall, practically glowing against the flowing gray of asphalt, brutalist architecture, and overcast sky.

"Huh?" Benji answered, temporarily unaware of his sweater. He'd glanced down, pinching his face in embarrassment. "Oh, yeah, me too." *Duh, why else would I be wearing it?* he thought.

"I'm Tara," she reached out a hand, hung it between them, and waited for him to meet it with his own. "We're neighbors. I followed you to school this morning."

"You did?" His hands had found their way into the pocket of his sweater, the warm fabric soothing him from the vulnerability of the revelation, until he noticed hers still hanging between them, still attempting to bridge the gap. He reached out and introduced himself.

"Hello, Benji," A giggle slipped through her lips as she answered him. "Yeah, until you cut into those woods. I thought maybe you were ditching class."

It was the first time he'd smiled at her. "No, it's a shortcut." He'd still been holding her hand, no longer shaking it. He let go, and his fist dug itself back into his pocket.

"Show me."

He agreed, and before long, Tara was following him through the woods, studying their surroundings with genuine excitement.

"Thanks for bringing me out here," Tara spoke, breaking through the whispering hum of the trees.

Benji forced himself to answer. "It's where I like to come to be alone." His eyes swept from thick oak trunks to prickly brambles and meager bushes. The words echoed through his mind, narrating his view with a newly discovered air of self-pity.

The wind picked up, howling through the surrounding forest and nipping at Benji and Tara's cheeks. Benji's sweater hugged him tightly, keeping him warm and safe from the late fall gloom. He noticed Tara wrapping her arms around her chest, attempting to hide her soft shivers.

"Take this," Benji choked out the words, gripping the sleeves of his sweater in his palms.

She hesitated, but he'd already begun to pull it off. He thrust it toward her, and she accepted it with grace.

Benji stared at the sweater, and he remembered. He remembered wearing it to the bank after working months at the Dollar General. He'd pinched every nickel and dime he earned, able to stop himself from spending any extra money on the movies and books that caught his eye. Even when he did buy, it was the used copies with tattered covers and faded art. It bothered him, but it was worth it. He'd left the bank that day with the statement pinched tightly between his fingers and his stomach warm with pride. He remembered drinking in the excitement of seeing $5,000 in print. It wasn't a fortune, but it was the closest he'd ever been to one. It was another step closer to college admissions. Another step closer to escaping Curry County.

He remembered bringing it home, sliding his bike past the Escort and up to the garage.

"Mom," he'd said, closing the front door behind him, the *click* from the latch echoing through the hall. "Mom, are you home?" Passing through the short and narrow hallway, he'd smelled the bittersweetness of a burning cigarette. He could still smell it now.

She sat at the dining room table, her face buried in her hands with the glowing ember pointing away from her like a beacon in the night.

"Mom?"

She'd lifted her face from her hands, her eyes puffy and red. "Hey, honey."

"Mom, what's wrong?"

"I, um," she struggled to get the words through her lips.

Benji remembered glancing at the table. A small gathering of white sheets tattooed in thin black print lay before her. He'd recognized the insignia printed across the top of the first sheet. It was the same symbol he'd recognized from his own trips to the doctor. He'd returned his gaze to hers, her eyes telling him more than her words ever could.

"I can help," he'd insisted, knowing what it meant for his fortune. "I'll work overtime, whatever I have to do. I'll pay for the treatment."

A ringing static filled the room. She answered him by placing the cigarette between her lips. The ember glowed and cast deep-pocketed shadows on her sunken cheeks. She pulled it away and inhaled a quick and shallow pocket of air. She hadn't wanted his help, or maybe she just doubted him. It had always been doubt. Doubt that he could be anything more than his father, doubt that he could do anything more than her. Only ever doubt. She blew a thick stream of smoke that billowed away from her before hanging in the room around them, unseen unless sought. The smoke would thin but never truly leave.

"I can help," he repeated. He hadn't meant to furrow his brows. He'd spent so much time learning to hide his frustrations, but here they were on full display.

"What're you gonna do?" She finally answered, her words acidic with vitriol. She ran the heel of her cigarette-less hand across her eyes, wiping away any remaining tears. "You can't help me. You can't even take care of yourself. I still do your laundry. I do your dishes. I pull your bike into the garage every night. You don't even have your license. How are you going to help me when you can't help yourself?"

Benji's lips sounded a quiet *pop* as his jaw fell, but he hadn't heard it. He hadn't felt the quickening thump of his heart as blood rushed through his body. He hadn't noticed his vision tunneling around her.

How could she say that? She doesn't let me do my laundry. She rushes to the sink before I have a chance to wash the dishes. She puts my bike away when I'm planning on leaving again. The thoughts raced through his mind until the words lost their meaning. Until he no longer thought in words but in shades of red and black.

"I can't help you," his voice echoed throughout the room in quivering reflection. "No one can help you because you won't help yourself. You're diagnosed with cancer, and what do you do? You smoke a pack of cigarettes. You might as well be celebrating."

Her face contorted as she leaned back in her chair. She looked as though he'd slapped her, stricken with disbelief, before quickly narrowing her eyes into predatory slits.

"No," he continued. "No, I can't help you because this is what you want. You deserve it, and you know it. You deserve everything you get."

Before she could respond, he turned and headed back down the hall to the front door. He needed to leave, needed to get away before the awful sting of shame forced him to apologize. That was what she wanted. She wanted him to feel sorry for her, or so he thought. He pulled the door toward him, quickly grabbing the outer handle and ripping it back into the frame behind him. It *banged* shut as he neared his bike. It had only been seconds before he was pedaling away from the house, swinging onto the road and distancing himself from her.

He wanted to burn the sweater. It was more than a reminder. It had become an object of curse that clung to him of his own accord. But he didn't believe that. He didn't believe anything. He didn't believe *in* anything. There was little room for faith in a life so punishing. He peeled his eyes away from the sweater and looked to his left, out the driver-side window that separated him from the downpour.

A candied red Tahoe sat parked a few spaces away. It was the only car in the lot that he recognized. Tara's parents' car. He'd rode in the backseat more times than he could count, sitting beside Tara, singing songs they knew by heart. It'd been years since he'd been in that car, but he could still remember the stained fabric seats and the artificial peony scent that fought to mask the mildewed floorboards.

Benji remembered riding in the back seat, Tara's dad blasting Disturbed and struggling to sing along. *Dad Rock.* That was what they'd called it. He would sing aloud, mumbling the majority of the lyrics while Tara turned bright red, trying and failing to hide her embarrassment. Humming along, he would just smile, unashamed by his ability to get along with her parents. He couldn't understand her embarrassment. In his dreams, it had been his father driving and half-heartedly singing.

The Tahoe had slowed to a stop in the park's parking lot, and Tara's dad waved them away. Together, the two disappeared into the woods they'd both grown so fond of.

"I wish I had my own car," Tara said.

"Why?" Benji started. "I like riding around with your dad. And your mom."

"They're *so* embarrassing."

Benji had given a knowing smile.

"Maybe you can buy a car." Tara returned his smile with her own, prodding with a light surge of smug sarcasm. "Now that you've got all that money."

His smile dipped into a look of dissatisfaction. "I'm saving for college."

"Then why'd you stay behind? You could be in Eugene right now. Grants aside, your GPA could get you a scholarship."

Fall term had started a week before, but he hadn't been quite ready to leave. It'd seemed right to spend another year saving. Another year with his best friend.

"I don't know," he'd answered. "I guess I felt bad leaving you behind." This was almost true.

"Yeah, yeah," Tara had answered with her typical tone of heartfelt dismissal.

"Hey," Benji had begun. "If you could be an animal, what would you be?"

Tara had lingered on the question for a moment, the seriousness in her eyes assuring him she was actually considering. It was the type of question that a child would ask, but he was no child and she knew he wouldn't have taken any answer but the truth. Her cheeks swelled as a smile grew across her face, and she glanced at him from the corner of her eye.

"I'd be a cat," she'd decided. "A lazy tabby who lays around all day, soaking in the sun and sleeping whenever and wherever I want."

Benji had held back his laughter, amused by her answer. It was fitting.

"Weird," he'd said. "I'd have taken you for a snake." They laughed, Tara giving him a soft shove.

"What about you? A slug or something?"

He rolled his eyes, his smile still stretching from ear to ear. Her comebacks had typically been bad, but they were worse when he teased her.

"I'd be a bird."

"Then I would have to hunt you!" With a makeshift claw, she'd raised her hand and swiped at him.

"I would fly away."

The two continued walking, passing great oak after great oak. They'd made their way through the forest until the trees thinned. The lake had laid before them, subtle and still. It had always managed to mesmerize them both, despite years of returning to that same spot. Trees reflecting in rotated Rorschaches evoked a deep sense of inner peace.

One of the twin doors at the face of the building swung out, and Tara's mother stepped through it. Steam plumed from her nose in a pair of twin streams that snaked down and away from her. Her eyes had locked onto him, and he knew she'd seen him from inside. He could tell from her puffy, pink eyes and pale, gaunt face that she'd only just stopped crying. It seemed to him that tears often came in waves, broken by brief moments of clarity that reared themselves in times of grief. He'd known grief well, from his time beside his mother in the hospital—he'd prepared himself to lose her, but she accepted his help and beat the cancer—but he couldn't comprehend the loss of an only child. It would have been natural to grieve a dead parent, and he'd long prepared himself for that moment. A moment that had yet to come.

He hadn't spoken with Tara since the night she told him about David. He wasn't jealous, but she didn't believe that. Or maybe he was, but it wasn't a romantic jealousy. He never liked David and knew Tara deserved better. She deserved better than Curry County. But she didn't see things that way.

"What is your deal?" Tara asked, her forehead creasing in ways Benji had never noticed before.

"He's a dick," Benji answered. "You deserve someone better than *David Parks*."

"You don't know what I deserve. I *like* him. I *like* him, Benji. You don't get to tell me what I deserve or who I should like."

Benji's stomach felt hollow and pitted. She was right, and for the first time, he saw her for what she was: *Human*. She was allowed to make her decisions and her *mistakes*. She was allowed to make mistakes, have fun, and feel sadness. She was allowed to feel and to *be*. His opinions about all of it were inconsequential. He didn't have any say over how she felt or acted. It was true, even if he didn't want it to be.

"Fine, you're right," Benji said. "But he's a dick, and you'll see for yourself. He'll cheat on you or hit you, or whatever he does, you'll see for yourself."

"I hate you." Her eyes went wide with surprise. She hadn't meant it—had she? It didn't matter, because, in that moment, it was true.

The woods went silent and motionless around them. Benji's jaw tightened, holding back every word he shouldn't say and every word he should. He turned away and began walking, leaving her to fade away in the darkness. It was the last time they spoke.

Benji watched Tara's mother as she stood in the doorway, looking back at him. He raised his hand at her, and she returned the motion with her own. Then his eyes began to ache, his jaw began to quiver, and the tears returned. It had been days since he cried, but there was no way to distract himself now. The only thing worse than facing the numbing cold of losing a friend was witnessing a parent face the reality of outliving their child. It was a cruel punishment unworthy of any crime. Yet, he saw a woman whose only crime was kindness. She would have bore the weight of the world for him, but he could never relieve this weight for her.

He couldn't get out of the car. He couldn't face the regret that dug itself deep inside of him. He'd lost her that night in the woods, but now she was gone.

What's lost can be found, but what's gone is gone.

Benji put the car in reverse and pulled away from the building, Tara's mother shrinking away from him through the rain-soaked windshield. He slipped the car into drive and sped away through the rain and tears.

It wasn't long after their fight that he returned to that same place in the woods, where the trees thinned. Gravel crunched beneath his feet like crushed ice, rough jags of stone grinding against stone. The gravel pressed up against his feet through the worn soles of his shoes. Each step brought him closer to Lake of the Woods, a stagnant, near-black sheet of impenetrable depth. Its surface reflected the setting sun, glowing an angry red. It was as red as blood.

Benji watched the water, studied every ripple, and imagined the jealous bodies that slithered and schooled within it. He resented the water for them and only vaguely felt grateful that they were confined to it, unable to crawl across the rock and swarm him where he stood. The thought made him shiver and sent a chill down his spine. He looked away from the water, his eyes darting across the branches that hung above the water's edge. They hung above the water like hands reaching, reaching, reaching, but never grabbing. Or maybe they were simply waiting, a threatening gesture, strong-arming the water to keep it where it lay.

His mind had strayed beyond its natural limit, and the lake was no longer a symbol of comfort. It had never been. Just as the water reflected the sun, the lake, its shore, and the surrounding trees were a reflection of who he was. He had been the trees, had been the angry sun glaring its blinding light off of the water's surface. He had been the jagged stones that prodded the soft pads of intruding feet. Where some arms reached to comfort, his were sharpened to points. Where blood might stain the water, slowly dissipating and spreading, he colored it infinitely. Where marble was smooth and silky, he was jagged and grinding. One thing had always been certain and always been known: the world was not his, but he was for the world. There was no talking his way out of it. It was time he accepted it, that like the lake—and like his mother—he was unmoving and immovable. He was shifting but ultimately unchanged. And there were no words that could change that.

Now, the wipers swept across the windshield, briefly clearing it of the rain. It was all a blur. The yellow-dotted lines in the road stuttered and flashed into a solid as the Escort sped. There was nowhere to go but forward and away, but he could never escape. He couldn't escape the death of his friend, the ruling thumb of his mother, or the claustrophobic stronghold of Curry County. The trees on either side of him rushed by in unfocused blends of green and brown and orange, all smudged in gray.

Ahead, he saw the forest to his right drop away and the ocean stretched out. He sped beside it, but it seemed to stand completely still. The base of the gas pedal met the floor and the car's engine pushed itself to keep up. Benji fought to break away. Just as his eyes returned to the windshield, he watched as a pair of bright red stars burst into his view. It was too close and he was moving too fast. The wheel pulled to the right and he felt the car push effortlessly through the old metal barrier.

For the first time in his life, he was weightless. He was flying.

The Attic

Su-Ling Dickinson

The resonance of a rolling thunderstorm
makes its presence known in my attic
as if all of the memories wanted to burst open
and break free from the chest that bound
them tightly to their owner

the rain pours into the decaying wood planks
a reminder to not die of consumption
of nostalgia and romance
because it all gets recycled
into secondhand trauma that drugs can't cure

windows begin to splinter
growing spindly legs breach the surface
washing away the silence and the rupture
that follows when god cracks a whip in the sky
childhood floating across the flooded room
screaming out for the attention

I can still see the small girl on these walls
collecting everything to make her whole again
but everything washes away like the peeling of skin

that has been weathered by the radiating sun
her mouth tries to move but she's a mannequin
controlled and restrained

it rains up here to trap all of the stories inside
the thunder drowns out the conversations
we knew we could have instead of martyrdom
grandma's thimble collection rolls around my feet
as I float away, high on nostalgia's destruction
I'm ready to be free

Reasons

Matthew J. Spireng

Don't get caught on foot
out in the middle of the
25-square-mile field

with a violent thunderstorm
moving in fast, faster than
you can run two-and-a-half miles

to your car. Advice worth
taking to heart, though you might
ask why you would walk

two-and-a-half miles
into the field on a summer day,
or any day, for that matter.

What could possibly draw you
out there? Think about that.
Amazing, isn't it, all

the reasons you can
come up with when you
really start to think about it.

Meanwhile, if you're out there
it might be time to find
a little dip in your surroundings

and lie down and prepare
for a show like none
you've ever witnessed before,

which, if you're brave and
a little crazy, is about as good
a reason as I can think of

to be out there in the middle
of a 25-square-mile field alone
with a violent storm approaching fast.

In These Last Days

Shelly Krehbiel

I am tired of writing the deaths
because they are all I can see.
I can't remember how your face looks
in the sunlight or what it sounds like
when you are laughing.

Ocean has been so far away.
Today I have come where I can see it,
taste its memory, feel wind, where I can
remember saying your name out loud
where you could hear me.

I want to give you lifes. I mean that
misspelling. I mean holding life
over and over, speaking like that,
each name containing its own
beginning and end.

There are so many now. I don't want
to blend them or leave any out,

each complete and part of something
larger than *lives*, which is also an action,
an always that doesn't stop.

Stopping matters.

Doesn't it feel good, my loves,
lifes in the mouth, the *f* and *s* blending
into a kind of wind, breath slipping
into the world instead of *v* vibrating
into *z*, descending.

See how the waves move here?
How there is so much sky?

A Little Bit Like Goldilocks

Elise Chadwick

It began with limber backs stacked
against cinder block walls. Limbs
tangled in soggy sheets pulling loose
from the dorm room mattress.
We breathed and dreamed as one.

That Spring we graduated to *Metro North*
commutes and late-night lesson planning.
Shared dreams whispered before tossing
lost in the quilt covered enormity
of our dimpled full-sized bed.

But then the babies came. The first
a milky breathed bundle of sighs,
the second, an acrobatic sleeper
and the bed no longer sufficed.

We ordered king-size for the cathedral
ceilinged room overlooking the Hudson.
Bookcases built in and pickled wood floors.
Room enough for bedtime stories,
midnight terrors and hazy hued sunsets.

Now, nearly lost to each other
in the emptiness of that big bed,
eyes closed, I reach across the expanse
and touch the soft heat of your dreams.

A Catalog I Kept Until

Cecil Morris

the roly-poly bugs that no longer rolled
themselves into tiny gray marbles,
the squirrels a shade or two lighter than the pavement,
the skunks redolent, the raccoons less furtive
and frightening flattened, squashed frogs and toads,
the umber crawdads who refused to live
in galvanized buckets in the backyard,
the flies wings down on window sills or caught in webs
where all buzzing ceased, the spiders with legs curled
around their secret, the birds a mere dust
of feathers under the tree, some cat's handiwork,
the valley gull wedged in chrome-colored grill,
one wing still spread as if in flight from death,
an endless string of trout, head-bashed, wide-eyed,
then gutted and rinsed clean by the creek's edge,
that spot in the intersection, the stain,
the melted melded sucker where we looked
and did not look as we waited for the bus
when school started again, the boy's family
we never saw again though their two cars
remained and new chain-link fencing circled

their front yard that fall, the two framed photos
on our mantle: my older brothers looking
serious in their matching green Class As

Another Time, Another Place

Abhishek Mehta

I see my mother tell small, harmless lies
on the phone sometimes.
Another time, another place,
doing something arbitrary with herself.
Slides her slim fingers under the dusty truth
and holds it just a few inches above the ground.
Airing it out like a carpet in August,
so that the damp underside of it
becomes less unbearable to think of.
Part of me thinks she wants
to be found out in one of her lies.
That someone should enter the room
when she's peeking under there,
not say anything, just look at her
and how burdened she is
with the care of an old carpet.
Another part of me imagines she's lifting it
higher and higher each day,
bowing her head little by little.
She has scraped out of her lies a time and a place
she can escape to.
Nobody knows she was *there, then.*

I keep expecting to walk into her room
to find her underneath the carpet.
Sweaty, swaddled in truth.
Dust motes from her shifting lump on the floor,
riding up a beam of sunlight from the window.
Making constellations too ordinary for the sky.

To Our Fault

Trish Sissons

I wasn't ready when the shaking began. To be fair, I don't think any-one was; it's just that I was in the precarious position of being perched on a rather exposed summit. As the mountain lurched and jolted be-neath me, my snowshoes failed to keep me upright. I fell and pressed myself flat against the face of the mountain like a starfish holding tight to whatever roots and rocks my fingers could find in the snow.

We were all well-aware that the Big One was looming and that one day, inevitably and invariably, our city would be destroyed. We all knew that Richmond would sink, swallowed up in silt, and that the wave would drown our downtown core. We'd been told our whole lives that we were overdue for it; that we Cascadians—with the hubris to build so much on a subduction zone—were living on borrowed time. And yet, the endless indoctrination of childhood earthquake drills and warnings from San Francisco did little to prepare us.

As my face and hands went numb, I lamented that there was no desk nor doorframe for me to brace under. In all of the scenarios that had played out in my head, I was at work or school, and it was certain-ly never winter. I suppose plate tectonics have little regard for seasons.

I opened my eyes in time to see the explosion of the pipeline under Mount Burnaby and the fall of Harbour Centre. I watched as the wall of water surged, eclipsing the remains of the sea wall, its white noise harmonizing with the tsunami sirens I didn't know the city had.

It looked like a tilt shift motion capture film of absurd and abstract destruction; it all happened far away, frame by frame.

My parents were in an earthquake once. They were at some jungle retreat in the lush mountains of Costa Rica. The shaking woke them and sent them running out into the night as it destroyed the animal sanctuary next door. While my father rallied to go back into the hotel to raid the mini bar for supplies, my mother curled up on the ground between the fissure cracks in the concrete, trying not to think about the snakes, or the child who'd been working in the now-destroyed tienda across the parking lot from her a few hours earlier.

They spent the night joking with their neighbors until they were airlifted out. It became their best dinner party anecdote, growing more colorful and daring with every retelling. My father would paint himself as a marauding hero, doing what it took to survive the night. He did not mention the people who were not invited to leave with them on the helicopters. "What bad timing," people said. "Such an unfortunate vacation for you. So, what happened next?"

In a lull between the aftershocks, I push myself up on shaky arms and delayed useful action with thoughts of future dinner parties.

I will be sitting at the table, leaning back in my chair with a glass of Shiraz in hand and, when pressed, I'll shake my head, *no, no, I couldn't possibly.* The guests will then goad me into it and the host will get it started and I'll roll my eyes and smile and correct them and say, *that's not how it happened.*

I'll focus my retelling on my survival skills; how I built a lean-to and melted snow for drinking water, waiting above the city for the dust to settle and the fires to burn themselves out. I will get a good laugh at my line about how I started to consider squirrels as a more desirable food source than my strictly rationed granola bars.

They'll ask if I was scared and I'll say no. I will get glassy-eyed and vague then, and think of the missing house and my missing people when I finally came down from the mountain after the water had receded and the stadiums had filled with tents. I will debate mentioning the wave that destroyed the Pacific Rim, or the liquefaction that swallowed people up whole. I will start, then pause when I see my father wink and tell me never to let the truth get in the way of a good story.

Stillness settles in on the mountain top and I shake my head and look down to the alpine meadow below, scanning for sticks to make fire and shelter. If I want to tell a survival story, I suppose I must survive first.

Writing and Drawing

Priscilla Long

The poet writes in a room
in a century where god is dead
and dinner late. She's here alone
with the page, tossed about
like scrap-paper, no one
to rescue her from the news
of guts spilled from gunshot wounds
or the death of democracy, or, it may be,
poetry. But writing rescues the evening,
for writing quiets the mind, the same
as drawing, as in that film of John Berger
listening to Tilda Swinton in the kitchen
while drawing her face. She peels an apple.
They speak of fathers not speaking
of what they know of war:
how long it takes for a soldier,
once he has been shot dead, to die.

Imposible

(original poem from The Dickinson Archive,
Spanish language, Argentina)

María Negroni

Hubiera querido ser la Abeja Reina. La Soberana que diseña el mundo en su dicción pasiva. Y después, apuesta a un tiempo que viene, que parte, y urde lo que debe, recostada en la miel callada que escribe no escribiendo, y vuelve antífona todo lo que toca.

Impossibility

(translated poem, English language)

Allison A. deFreese (translator)

I would have liked to be Queen Bee. The Sovereign who plans the world in her passive diction. Later, she wagers a time that arrives—then leaves—and plots what she must, reclining in the silent honey that writes by not writing, and turns everything she touches into antiphony.

Putting the Dog Down

Kimberly Nunes

Though it meant death
the van pulled up in luminous sun
though it meant death—
carried to sand, her final ocean whiff
kind eyes on us, haunches stilled,
a big heart too large, and all this beauty—
though it meant death

Containers for Sun

Angela Townsend

Cats do not need to "come to their senses," because they never left.

I keep wandering off.

I share my life with improbable brown pom-poms who know their place upon the earth. When the axis shifts and the hour gleams, they become containers for sun. They report to the window because they are light and matter. They are wise enough to listen to their molecules.

I forget to listen to music.

I have decorated my cerebrum so plushily, I never want to leave. The tufted velvet sofa holds me like a lap, and brocades boast so much gold, the sun seems redundant. My head is so homey, I would say it smells like banana bread, if only I had brought my nose.

I trade scent for the comforts of home, and my address is interior.

I am not alone in living like a lollipop with the sweetness stored upstairs. My heady loves and I visit each other's bungalows, complimenting the interior design. No one notices if the tea is weak. I trip over my toes on the way out, then need to look up "toes" to remember what they are and why they wiggle.

But cats sprint across my path, startling me like the comets who played Tag in grade school.

I watched them buzz and read essays on honey. My solemn lollipop best friend sat beside me on the hill, expounding on Hobbit sociology and tearing his sandwich into smaller and smaller nubbins. The closest we got to the Tag team was the day Ben ascended the monkey bars for the sole purpose of singing *Man of La Mancha* songs with appropriate intensity.

He almost fell. I almost fell downstairs into my ears.

Meanwhile, cats chase and taste, keeping up correspondence with the warp and weft of the world.

Perhaps this is why I lash myself to these shag Buddhas like grappling hooks. It may be no coincidence that my infatuation with cats chased my diabetes diagnosis at age nine. I filled my bony arms with an elf as red as embarrassment, the gentlest clown in the shelter.

Figgy sniffed out the vital signs of my childhood, proclaiming me a living creature. I buried my face in his fur and sketched the shape of his eyes. I savored his senses, bringing in crystal snowballs for his assessment. We ran circles through the living room, whirling containers for delight. I put a star-shaped kibble in my mouth just to learn what Figgy knew.

But wisdom is more fragile than knowledge, and adolescence is a violent city for the senses. The body was a discotheque of unsavory characters. I would not let them catch me.

I put the stars back in the encyclopedia, then boxed it in the basement. I read until my legs fell asleep. I wrote until not even my grandmother's plural *parmigianas* could rouse me.

I worried and walloped myself with words unheard. I painted worst-case scenarios.

I felt axes twirl and angers explode my electrons. I had no container for them.

My loneliest lollipop years came in campus housing, a sensory deprivation tank permitting "only such pets as may safely and humanely fit within a terrarium."

Sturdier classmates crunched peanuts and navigated nougat, chasing Zydeco parties and shiny bodies and quad grass and other grass. I subsisted on pieces of theses, affirmations exuding neither odor nor vapor.

When I clumsily knocked down a ceramic angel in my dorm room and her head snapped clean off, I lay on the floor gripping it like the earth's last hazelnut. I cried until I tasted salt.

Ninety miles away, Figgy died. I was not there, left only with watercolor dreams of his ascension.

But Figgy never left.

Figgy summoned the coming cavalry, the cats who would come in numbers too comical for any clown. Where I had assumed I would adopt a pet instantly after graduation, I chased no dreams of working among cats full-time.

But love is a wry author of lives, and my body bumbled into a vocation of veins and tails. Within a year, I would be the Development Director for a sanctuary housing one hundred cats. Sixteen years later, four thousand of them have been my personal bodhisattvas.

When they are angry, they gnash their teeth like the Bible's damned. When they are hungry, they smack their lips like lotharios. When they surge with love, they settle for nothing short of touch, fingers raking their ribs like gardens of Eden.

They are containers of grace because they have no hostages in the attic. All four thousand have been greedy for more senses, more bawdy downstairs galoots swinging their steins and singing their limericks. They are holy wholeness, chasing every candy color of a world made to be consumed.

They are astute, these tortoiseshell psychologists and flamepoint social workers. They smell burning neuroses and pivot accordingly. When they cannot chase me to the chaotic dining hall, they will lure me by the force of their own needs.

Follow us into this trapezoid of sun. Lay down. Further down. Rub this neglected ear. Now the other one. Soft, yes? Good.

Stay awhile. Just stay. Just stop. No words. Not this time.

Hold me. Feel weight. Hear this yawp. Hear yourself laugh. Silly, yes? Good.

Be close. Be vital. Be here.

Their address is everywhere.

They address me as a living creature.

My signs may be vital yet.

Heart of the Tongass IV

Mark Holian

All day rain on island hills
  of spruce and hemlock
  cedar aspen berry bushes
  fills the ears with small percussions
  loosening sounds impacted there
  and dissipates sorrow with
  the sound of water filling a forest
  on its way to the sea

it's all wet the dripping
  arms and leaves of devil's club
  dwarf dogwood splayed on sphagnum
  blades of bent beach grass

  few sticks in low tide mud a
  thousand year old Tlingit fish trap
  shows the path of ancient salmon
      by the mouth of a swollen rill
      run down from bare rock heights
      through muskeg pools
      ringed with shore pine
      eclectic bog flowers

into old growth forest rooms
and exit on barnacled beach rocks
kelp and clam mud flats
slips into tidal flow
showing something like acceptance

Ekphrasis 16: "Untitled (Expulsion)," Fred Tomaselli, 2000

John Blair

Imagine a man and a woman separated
by divine will from the divine itself
how they stand together in their abstract
trepidation about What Awaits Us Out There
stranded on a horizonless plain of grass and stars
side by side like stones like exceptions in
and of themselves as baroque as any real number
who together exist as Platonic ideals of everything
that limits us to our vulnerable inevitable selves
and say that this day that they're living is every day
that's worth living wholly to its end and when
that end comes these two will be nothing more
than clouds of fraught probabilities slashes
in the fabric of a bright black sky statistical
accidents like wind or waves or love their bodies
a kind of Thou and I disguised as light
disguised as enumerations of births and deaths
as blood and nerves as abstract suns as pyres
waiting to be lit in the now and always now

that is all the moments in which they stand
mid-step for the sake of us all afraid
of this life and every other that no one
ever asked them to live.

Contributors

Carolina Atkins is a writer based in West Tennessee. She is a lover of folklore, theatre, and French literature. She worked as the historical researcher for a production of Molière's *Tartuffe*, and is currently working on an English translation of Eugène Ionesco's *Le Roi se meurt*. Her previous work has appeared in *Living Waters Review*.

Devon Balwit walks in all weather and has recently returned to life-drawing and cartooning with great joy. Her most recent collection is *Spirit Spout* (Nixes Mate Books, 2023.)

Craig Beaven is the author of four collections of poetry, most recently *In Arcadia* (Rane Arroyo Chapbook Series, Seven Kitchens Press) and *Teaching the Baby to Say I Love You* (Anhinga Press Poetry Prize). His work appears in *Hollins Critic*, *Beloit Poetry Journal*, *Western Humanities Review*, *Prairie Schooner*, and many others.

Jake Bienvenue holds an MFA from the University of Montana, where he was the Editor-in-Chief of *CutBank*. He is at work on a novel about the wine industry in Oregon's Willamette Valley.

John Blair as published poems with various magazines, including *Poetry*, *The Sewanee Review*, *The Georgia Review*, *The Colorado Review*, and *New Letters*.

Ace Boggess is author of six books of poetry, most recently *Escape Envy*. His writing has appeared in *Indiana Review, Michigan Quarterly Review, Notre Dame Review, Hanging Loose*, and other journals. An ex-con, he lives in Charleston, West Virginia, where he writes and tries to stay out of trouble. His seventh collection, *Tell Us How to Live*, is forthcoming in 2024 from Fernwood Press.

Chuck Carlise was born on the first Flag Day of the Jimmy Carter Administration, and has lived in 14 states and two continents since. He is the author of the collection *In One Version of the Story* (New Issues) and the chapbooks *A Broken Escalator Still Isn't the Stairs* and *Casual Insomniac*. His poems and essays can be found at *Pleiades, Diagram, Southern Review, Nimrod, Verse Daily, Best New Poets*, and elsewhere. He lives in Cleveland, Ohio, and directs the Ashland Poetry Press.

Elise Chadwick taught English at Horace Greeley High School in Chappaqua, NY, for 30 years. She lives in NYC but draws much inspiration for her poems from the time she spends upstate NY in her 200 year old home coexisting with the deer, groundhog, fox, bats, rabbits and squirrels, who got there first. Her poems have been recently published in *The Ocotillo Review, Healing Muse, Naugatuck River Review, The English Journal*, and others.

Janelle Cordero is an interdisciplinary artist and educator living in Spokane, WA. Her writing has been published in dozens of literary journals, including *Harpur Palate, Autofocus*, and *Hobart*, while her paintings have been featured in venues throughout the Pacific Northwest. Janelle is the author of four books of poetry, including *Impossi-*

ble Years (V.A. Press, 2022). Her forthcoming collection, *Talk Louder*, will be published in April 2024 with Papeachu Press.

Riley Danvers is a bisexual and disabled poet living in Portland, Oregon. Her poetry has been published in *Z Publishing House*, *Silkworm*, *Clackamas Literary Review*, *Other Worldly Women Press*, *Chasing Shadows*, *Wingless Dreamer Publication*, *Poets Choice* and *Fox Paw Literary Blog*. Other poems will be featured in the forthcoming anthology *MOSAIC*, releasing in 2024. Riley graduated with her M.F.A. in Poetry from Willamette University in 2021, and completed her M.A. in Literature from Mercy College in 2023. Her debut book of poetry, *Even the Air, Too Heavy*, was published by First Matter Press in 2022.

Holly Day's poetry has recently appeared in *Analog SF*, *Cardinal Sins*, and *New Plains Review*, and her published books include *Music Theory for Dummies* and *Music Composition for Dummies*. She currently teaches classes at The Loft Literary Center in Minnesota, Hugo House in Washington, and The Muse Writers Center in Virginia.

Allison A. deFreese is an instructor in CCC's English Department. Her translations of María Negroni's work have been shortlisted for Asymptote's Close Approximations Prize and appear in *CAGIBI*, *The Common*, *The Festival Review*, *Poetry Northwest*, and *Sequestrum*. Her recent book translations include María Negroni's *Elegy for Joseph Cornell* (Dalkey Archive Press, 2020). The Dickinson Archive is forthcoming from Dalkey Archive Press and Deep Vellum Publishing in 2025.

Su-Ling Dickinson is a 36-year-old writer and artist in the Portland, Oregon area. Her writing has appeared in *The Bond Street Review*,

Breathe Bold Magazine, and several indie literary journals. Su-Ling enjoys being a total cinephile, photography, and "a damn fine cup of coffee." Her writing is inspired by raw emotion, cultural collision, and latent content.

Cat Dixon is the author of *What Happens in Nebraska* (Stephen F. Austin University Press, 2022) along with six other poetry chapbooks and collections. She is a poetry editor with *The Good Life Review*. Recent poems published in *The Book of Matches*, *North of Oxford*, *hex*, and *The Southern Quill*.

Abbie Doll is a writer residing in Columbus, OH, with an MFA from Lindenwood University and is a Fiction Editor at Identity Theory. Her work has been featured in *Door Is a Jar Magazine*, *Full House Literary*, and *The Bitchin' Kitsch*, among others.

Rosemarie Dombrowski (RD) is the inaugural Poet Laureate of Phoenix, AZ, the founding editor of rinky dink press, and the founding director of Revisionary Arts, a nonprofit that facilitates self-care and healing through poetry. She's the recipient of a Laureate Fellowship from the Academy of American Poets, the winner of the 2017 *Split Rock Review* chapbook competition, and the author of three collections of poetry. Her work has appeared in *Poetry Daily*, *poets.org*, at the Emily Dickinson Museum, on local NPR affiliates, national NPR podcasts, the TEDx stage, and elsewhere. RD is a Teaching Professor at Arizona State University, the founding editor of *ISSUED: Stories of Service*, and the creator of Verse for Vets, a poetic medicine program for veterans supported by the Office for Veteran and Military Academic Engagement at ASU.

Linda Drach is a poet, public health program analyst, and volunteer writing group facilitator for the nonprofit Write Around Portland. Her poetry has been published in *CALYX*, *Cathexis Northwest*, *The Write Launch*, *Clackamas Literary Review*, *The Timberline Review*, and elsewhere. She lives and works in Oregon and studies at the Writers Studio.

Dion Farquhar has recent poems in *New Words Press*, *Black Fox Review*, *Non-Binary Review*, *Superpresent*, *Blind Field*, *Poesis*, *Cape Rock: Poetry*, *Mortar*, *Local Nomad*, *Columbia Poetry Review*, *moria*, *Shifter*, *BlazeVOX*, etc. Her third poetry book just out from Finishing Line Press, and she has three chapbooks. She works as an exploited adjunct at two universities, but is still learning from her students. She is active in the University of California Santa Cruz adjunct union, the UC-AFT.

Melvin Louis Fessler was born on May 8, 1945, in Phillipsburg, Kansas. After serving in the US Navy for five years, he lovingly endured 35 years of homemade treats left in mailboxes while working for the US Post Office. There was not a soul who knew Mel without his camera in hand and a sparkle of mischief in his eye. His life was spent primarily outdoors with his family, capturing both beautiful photos of the natural world and horrifically embarrassing candid shots of his loved ones. After his passing on November 23, 2021, Mel left behind a legacy of love, kindness, creativity, and more photos than his family knows what to do with.

Michael J. Galko is a scientist and poet who lives and works in Houston, TX. He was a 2019 Pushcart Award nominee, a finalist in the

2020 *Naugatuck River Review* narrative poetry contest, and a finalist in the 2022 *Bellevue Literary Review* poetry contest. In the past year he has had poems published or accepted at *North Dakota Quarterly, Epiphany, Eclectica, Louisville Review, Tar River Poetry,* and *Noon: journal of the short poem,* among other journals.

A Pushcart and Best of the Net nominated poet, **E. Laura Golberg's** work has appeared in *Rattle, Poet Lore, Barrow Street, Birmingham Poetry Review, RHINO,* and the *Journal of Humanistic Mathematics,* among other venues. She won first place in the Washington, DC Commission on the Arts Larry Neal Poetry Competition.

J Kramer Hare is a native of Pittsburgh, PA, where he lives and writes. When not reading or writing he enjoys rock climbing and listening to jazz. His work has appeared or is forthcoming in *Uppagus, the Ulu Review, The Road Not Taken, Jerry Jazz Musician, Untenured, Quibble Lit,* and *Millennial Pulp.*

Suzy Harris lives in Portland, OR. Her poems have appeared in *Calyx, Clackamas Literary Review,* and *Switchgrass Review,* among other journals and anthologies. Her chapbook *Listening in the Dark,* about hearing loss and learning to hear again with cochlear implants, was published by The Poetry Box in February 2023.

Mark Holian, former Alaskan resident, lives, and writes, and reads quite a bit in northern California. His poems have appeared in *The Banyan Review* and *Permafrost.* He walks frequently for physical and mental health.

Matthew Kohut has worked as a writer, teacher, and musician. His poetry has appeared or is forthcoming in *Tar River Poetry*, *Psaltery & Lyre*, *River Heron Review*, and *Wild Roof Journal*, among other publications. He is the co-author of two books of nonfiction.

Shelly Krehbiel holds an MFA from Antioch University Los Angeles. Her poems have appeared in publications such as *Lunch Ticket*, *The Midwest Quarterly*, and *The Fourth River*. She comes from Kansas and now lives in Eugene, Oregon, where she is steward to a garden, its wonderous beings, and two extraordinary cats.

Joshua Kulseth earned his BA in English from Clemson University, his MFA in poetry from Hunter College, and his PhD in poetry from Texas Tech University. His poems have appeared and are forthcoming in *Tar River Poetry*, *The Emerson Review*, *The Worcester Review*, *Rappahannock Review*, *The Windhover*, and others. His poetry manuscript, *Leaving Troy*, was shortlisted for the *Cider Press Review* Publication Competition.

Git Lanza lives in Bogota, Colombia. His poems have appeared occasionally in literary magazines in the U.S.

Eric le Fatte was educated at MIT and Northeastern University in biology and English. He has worked correcting catalog cards in Texas, and as the Returns King at Eastern Mountain Sports, but currently hikes, writes, teaches, and does research on tiny things in the Portland, OR area. He has published poems in *Rune*, *The Mountain Gazette*, *The Poeming Pigeon*, *The Raven Chronicles*, *Windfall*, *Verseweavers*, *US#1 Worksheets*, *Perceptions*, *Cirque*, *Clade Song*, *Clover*, *Tiny*

Seed, Deep Wild, Canary, and happily enough, a while ago in *The Clackamas Literary Review.*

Priscilla Long is a Seattle-based writer of poetry, creative nonfiction, science, history, and fiction, and a long-time independent teacher of writing. Her seventh book is *Dancing with the Muse in Old Age* (Coffeetown, 2022). Her two poetry books are *Holy Magic* (MoonPath Press) and *Crossing Over: Poems* (University of New Mexico Press). Her awards include a National Magazine Award and ten of her essays have been honored as "notable" in various years of Best Essays.

Natalie Marino is a poet and physician. Her work appears in *Pleiades, Rust + Moth, Salt Hill, South Florida Poetry Journal,* and elsewhere. She is the author of the chapbook *Under Memories of Stars* (Finishing Line Press, 2023). She lives in California.

Trapper Markelz (he/him) writes from Arlington, MA. He is the author of the chapbook *Childproof Sky,* a Cherry Dress Chapbooks 2023 selection. His work has appeared in the journals *Baltimore Review, Dillydoun Review, Wild Roof Journal, Greensboro Review,* and *Passengers Journal,* among others.

Steven Mayer, PhD, MBA, started writing after he retired from the University of Oregon and an extensive business management career. His education and professions matter less than the amazing people who have touched his life. Steve and his wife Linda moved to the North Oregon Coast in 2016. He has published three books, the *Finding Heart* series, of memoir, nonfiction, creative nonfiction, and poetry, and his writing appears in various Northwest literary journals. He enjoys being an armchair philosopher, storyteller, adventurer, sports enthusiast, and beach wanderer.

Abhishek Mehta is a marketing professional from India with a discreet passion for putting words together in a way that they may be able to hold his short and sudden glances in their direction every now and then. His writing has previously appeared and is forthcoming in *Dunes Review*, *Inkwell Journal*, and *South Florida Poetry Journal*.

Darren Montufar is a writer living and working in Des Moines, IA. Outside of spending time with family and friends, he enjoys exploring fiction, photography, and the great outdoors.

After 37 years of teaching high school English, **Cecil Morris** has turned his attention to writing poetry. He has poems appearing or forthcoming in *Cimarron Review*, *Ekphrastic Review*, *Hole in the Head Review*, *Rust + Moth*, *Sugar House Review*, and *Talking River Review*. He and his indulgent partner, mother of their children, divide their time between the arid Central Valley of California and the cooler coast of Oregon.

Maya Muir spent her professional life as a freelance journalist, book reviewer, and school administrator, while writing fiction on the side, and recurrently turning to poetry. Only in the last few years has she been able to truly apprentice to the practice of poetry. She's lived in Philadelphia, New York, Boston, and Los Angeles, but now has deep roots in Portland, in the wonderfully varied and beautiful state of Oregon. She has a passion for the diversity of places, languages and peoples, and words. Always words. She has published in *The Ravens Perch*, *Ohio Woman*, *Calyx*, and the *Green Mountains Review*.

María Negroni (Rosario, Argentina) has published over 20 books, including poetry, nonfiction and novels. *Islandia, Night Journey, Andanza* (The Tango Lyrics), *Mouth of Hell*, and *The Annunciation* have appeared in English, and her work has also been translated into Swedish, Portuguese, Italian, and French. María Negroni received a Guggenheim fellowship for poetry in 1994, a Rockefeller Foundation fellowship in 1998, the Fundación Octavio Paz fellowship for poetry in 2001, and The New York Foundation for the Arts fellowship in 2005. She also received a National Book Award for her collection of poems *El viaje de la noche*, a PEN Award for *Islandia* as best book of poetry in translation (New York 2001), and the Premio Internacional de Ensayo y Narrativa de Siglo XXI for her book *Galería Fantástica*. She taught at Sarah Lawrence College from 1999 to 2014, and is now director of Argentina's first creative writing program, at Universidad Nacional de Tres de Febrero.

Kimberly Nunes's poems have been published in *The Alembic, Apricity Magazine, Avalon Literary Review, Blue Light Press Anthology, Brushfire, California Quarterly, Caveat Lector, El Portal, Evening Street Review, Flights, Mantis, Marin Poetry Center Anthology, The Madison Review,* OPEN: *A Journal of Arts & Letters, The Round, Spotlog Review, Sweet: A Literary Confection, Whimperbang, WomenArts Quarterly Journal,* and *Adelaide Literary Magazine*. Her poem "Morning at Moore's Lake, Again" was nominated for the 2022 Pushcart Prize. She has attended numerous writing workshops and studied with Marie Howe, Sharon Olds, Ellen Bass, and many others. Kimberly sits on the board of Four Way Books in New York City. She received her MFA in poetry from Sarah Lawrence College. Her hobbies include bird-watching, gardening, swimming, golf, and tennis.

Gillian Reimann is a passionate writer with a background in both fantasy and memoir writing. With a Bachelor's of Arts degree in Creative Writing from Pacific University and a Master's of Fine Arts degree from Saint Mary's College of California, she has experience with both the academic and more pop-culture aspect of writing with fanfiction. With inspiration taking her across every genre and form of writing she never knows where she's going to end up next.

Mary Rohrer-Dann is author of *Accidents of Being: Poems from a Philadelphia Neighborhood* (Kelsay Books, 2023); *Taking the Long Way Home*; and *La Scaffetta: Poems from the Foundling Drawer*. Her flash collection, *Meanwhile, in the Hungry Dark...* is currently seeking a home. Her work has appeared most recently in *Flash Boulevard, Literary Mama, Slant, Five South, Orca, Clackamas Literary Review, Indiana Review*, and *Comstock Review*. She paints, hikes, bikes, sometimes gardens, and volunteers with various nonprofits in central PA.

Ellen Sazzman is a Pushcart-nominated poet whose work has been recently published in *Atlanta Review, Folio, Delmarva Review, Peregrine, Another Chicago, PANK, Ekphrastic Review, WSQ, Sow's Ear, Lilith, Common Ground*, and *CALYX*, among others. Her poetry collection *The Shomer* (2021) was selected as a finalist for the 2020 Blue Lynx Prize, and a semifinalist for the 2020 Elixir Press Antivenom Award and the 2019 Codhill Press Award. She was awarded first place in the 2022 Dancing Poetry Festival, received an honorable mention in the 2019 Ginsberg poetry contest, was shortlisted for the 2018 O'Donoghue Prize, and was awarded first place in Poetica's 2016 Rosenberg poetry competition.

Shawn Schenck (he/him) is an author and musician from Portland, OR. His writing includes elements of horror, the weird, crime, and fabulism. Shawn's work has been featured in the *Clackamas Literary Review* and *The Yard: Crime Blog*. He enjoys reading and watching films with his family. His favorite color is yellow.

Pattabi Seshadri's poems have appeared in *Beloit Poetry Journal, Cincinnati Review, American Letters & Commentary*, and other journals. He is an American of mixed (Indian and Jewish) heritage who grew up in Texas. He currently lives in San Francisco with his wife and daughter.

Vivek Sharma is a poet from the hills of the Mahabharata. They now reside in the unceded territory of the Syilx Okanagan peoples and pursue an MFA at the University of British Columbia. Their work juxtaposes and entangles life in two valleys and explores what it means to be a first-generation South Asian in the so-called Canada.

Eva-Maria Sher's poetry has appeared in *After Happy Hour Review, The Adirondack Review, Apricity Magazine, Big Scream, Bluestem, Brief Wilderness, Cadillac Cicatrix, California Quarterly, Cape Rock, DASH Literary Journal, Door Is A Jar Magazine, Dos Passos Review, Doubly Mad, Drunk Monkeys, East Jasmine Review, Euphony, Forge, Free State Review, Front Range Review, GW Review, Hawaii Pacific Review, The HitchLit Review, The Hollins Critic, I-70 Review, Ignatian Literary Review, ken*again, The MacGuffin, October Hill Magazine, Old Red Kimono, OxMag, The Paragon Journal, Penmen Review, Pennsylvania English, Perceptions Magazine, Poetic Sun, Poydras Review, Prism Review, riverSedge, Rougarou, Ship of*

Fools, Slag Review, Soundings East, Third Wednesday, Torrid Literature Journal, Umbrella Factory Magazine, Vending Machine Press, The Virginia Normal, Visitant, Westview, Willow Review, and *Your Impossible Voice.*

Trish Sissons is a BC-born writer currently based in Toronto. Her work has been shortlisted for the Fiddlehead's 2023 fiction contest and the 2020 Penguin Random House Student Award for Fiction.

Derek R. Smith (he/him) is a public health professional, Anishinaabe two-spirit, wanderer, who finds it hard to not write poetry. He has recent publications in *Great Lakes Review, San Pedro River Review, ¡Pa'lante!, euphony, Hearth & Coffin, Inlandia, Willawaw, Lucky Jefferson,* and others. There is no space for distance here, in poetry, and isn't that a beautiful thing?

Emma Snyder (BS, BA,) is a young writer living with chronic mental and physical illness, and like many, uses writing as a way to heal. She is the co-founder & Editor-In-Chief of *Tabula Rasa Review,* and her writing has been published or is forthcoming in the *Emerson Review, Furrow, Periphery, Abbey Review, Chimera Projects,* and *orangepeel mag.*

Matthew J. Spireng's 2019 Sinclair Poetry Prize-winning book *Good Work* was published by Evening Street Press. A 12-time Pushcart Prize nominee, he is the author of two other full-length poetry books, *What Focus Is* and *Out of Body,* winner of the 2004 Bluestem Poetry Award, and five chapbooks.

Geo. Staley is retired from teaching literature and writing at Portland Community College. He had also taught in New England, Appalachia, and on the Rosebud Sioux Indian Reservation. His poetry has appeared in *Chest, Main Street Rag, Blue Mountain Review, Clackamas Literary Review, RE:AL Artes Liberales, New Mexico Humanities Review, Fireweed, Trajectory, Evening Street Review, Slab*, and others.

Pacific Northwest writer **Scott T. Starbuck's** Trees, Fish, and Dreams Climateblog has readers in 110 countries, praised by editors Adeline Johns-Putra of Xi'an Jiaotong-Liverpool University, China, and Kelly Sultzbach of University of Wisconsin, La Crosse in The Cambridge Companion to Literature and Climate. He taught ecopoetry workshops the past five years at Scripps Institution of Oceanography in the UC San Diego Masters of Advanced Studies Program in Climate Science and Policy. His book *Bridge at the End of the World, New and Selected [Climate] Poems*, won a 2023 Blue Light Book Award, and his *Hawk on Wire*, chosen July 2017 as "Editor's Pick" at Newpages.com, was selected from over 1,500 books as a 2018 Montaigne Medal Finalist at Eric Hoffer Awards for "the most thought-provoking books."

Travis Stephens is a tugboat captain who lives and works in California. His book of poetry, *skeeter bit & still drunk* was published by Finishing Line Press.

Jeanine Stevens latest publications: *No Lunch Among the Day Stars*, (Cold River Press, 2022), and chapbooks, *Ornate Persona* (Clare Songbirds Publishing House, 2022) and *Tea in the Nun's Library*, (Eyewear

Publishing, UK 2022). She is winner of the MacGuffin Poet Hunt, WOMR Cape Cod Community Radio National Award, The Ekphrasis Prize, and The William Stafford Award. Jeanine has been published in *Evansville Review*, *North Dakota Review*, *Chiron Review*, *The Kerf*, and *Two Thirds North* (Sweden). Jeanine studied poetry at U.C. Davis, received her MA at CSU Sacramento and has a doctorate in Education. She is instructor at American River College.

Mark Sullivan's poetry and prose have appeared recently in *Cimarron Review*, *Lake Effect*, and *Tar River Poetry*. His first collection of poetry, Slag, received the Walt McDonald First Book Prize from Texas Tech University Press. He lives in New York City.

Angela Townsend is the Development Director at Tabby's Place: a Cat Sanctuary. She graduated from Princeton Seminary and Vassar College. Her work appears or is forthcoming in *Arts & Letters*, *Chautauqua*, *Paris Lit Up*, *The Penn Review*, *The Razor*, *Terrain.org*, and *The Westchester Review*, among others. She is a 2023 Best Spiritual Literature nominee. Angie has lived with Type 1 diabetes for 33 years, laughs with her poet mother every morning, and loves life affectionately.

Lee Varon is a social worker and writer. Her poetry and prose have been published in various journals including *Constellations*, *The Chamber Magazine*, *deLuge Literary and Arts Journal*, *Flights*, *Ibbetson Street*, and *Vagabond City Poetry*, among others. She has published a children's book, *My Brother is Not a Monster: A Story of Addiction and Recovery*.

Nickolai Vasilieff resides in a cabin along the Deschutes River in Oregon. As a Navy veteran, private pilot, father, and author, he traveled to over 40 countries, including a year-long global backpacking adventure. He worked as a marketing consultant for two decades, publishing numerous interviews, articles, and corporate profiles before venturing into novel writing. Nickolai penned the Empath series, targeting middle-grade/young adult readers with tales influenced by his international journeys and family vacations. His fascination with youthful imagination and thirst for adventure fuels his passion for young adult novels.

Ross West has placed fiction, essays, journalism, and poetry in publications from *Orion* to the *Journal of Recreational Linguistics*. His work has been anthologized in *Best Essays Northwest*, *Best of Dark Horse Present*, and elsewhere. He was editor-in-chief at the University of Oregon's research magazine, *Inquiry*; was senior managing editor at *Oregon Quarterly*; and served as text editor for the *Atlas of Oregon* and the *Atlas of Yellowstone*. "Smoke, Fire, Ashes" appears in his recently published collection of short stories *The Fragile Blue Dot*.

Phil Wetjen recently retired from a career in IT, where his role as a project manager allowed him to travel internationally, with extended assignments in Japan, China, and the UK. With retirement has come time for writing, including the editing of short stories based on his years living in the Pacific Northwest. Many of the events in these stories are based on the 'character building' jobs Phil had before embarking on his IT career.

Kelleen Zubick's work has appeared in a number of journals, including *Agni Online, Barrow Street, december, Dogwood, Many Mountains Moving, The Seattle Review, The Massachusetts Review, The Antioch Review,* and *Willow Springs.* She received an MFA in Creative Writing from Arizona State University and has been awarded artist residencies from the Anderson Center for Interdisciplinary Studies (MN) and from the Kimmel Harding Nelson Center for the Arts (NE). Kelleen lives with her family in Denver and works remotely as Managing Director, Early Childhood and Health Systems for the national No Kid Hungry campaign.

The *Clackamas Literary Review* is typeset in Sabon LT Std, an old-style serif designed by Jan Tschichold, and in Optima, a humanistic sans-serif designed by Hermann Zapf, and printed on 50 lb. creme paper. Editing and design done by English Department students and faculty at Clackamas Community College, in Oregon City, Oregon.

Visit

CLR
CLACKAMAS LITERARY REVIEW

clackamasliteraryreview.wordpress.com
clackamasliteraryreview.submittable.com
facebook.com/clackamasliteraryreview
@clackamaslitrev

Contact
clr@clackamas.edu

CLACKAMAS LITERARY REVIEW

the finest writing for the best readers

Clackamas Literary Review has been committed to publishing quality writing from around the world since 1997. Use the form below or visit us on Submittable to receive the latest and forthcoming issues.

Clackamas Literary Review

_____	1 year	$15
_____	2 years	$28
_____	3 years	$40

Name _____

Address _____

City / State / Zip _____

Email _____

Send this form and check or money order to:

Clackamas Literary Review
English Department
Clackamas Community College
19600 Molalla Avenue
Oregon City, Oregon 97045